The huge computer Colossus hummed and throbbed on the Isle of Wight, mechanically running Earth and its myriad operations. Was it Good? Was it Evil? The Sect worshipped Colossus as a God. The Fellowship opposed it as the Devil incarnate and sought to escape its domination. Two groups of Terrans were in mortal conflict.

And then a third group was heard from.

Because Colossus, grown more and more powerful, was extending its domain beyond the five continents of Earth . . .

And the Martians didn't like it.

By the Same Author

DENVER IS MISSING

THE FALL OF COLOSSUS

D. F. Jones

A BERKLEY MEDALLION BOOK
published by
BERKLEY PUBLISHING CORPORATION

For Pearl and Roger Ford

Library of Congress Catalog Card Number: 73-87195

SBN 425-04326-6

BERKLEY MEDALLION BOOKS are published by
Berkley Publishing Corporation
200 Madison Avenue
New York, N.Y. 10016

BERKLEY MEDALLION BOOKS ® TM 757,375

Printed in the United States of America

Berkley Medallion Edition, FEBRUARY, 1975
FOURTH PRINTING

I

CHARLES FORBIN, sometime Professor of Cybernetics of the Harvard-Princeton Combine and honorary PhD of more universities than he could begin to remember, stared across the short stretch of sea to the mist-shrouded shore of England, USE, lost in thought.

At this hour of the morning they were usually trivial, inconsequential thoughts; they were now. He was thinking that this promised to be one of those rare English days when the sun would really shine. In another hour the soft, luminous veil of mist would burn off, revealing in sharp clarity the face of this old, strange land. The locals would have looked at that mist, nodded sagely, and told each other that they were "in for a real scorcher." Would have; not any more. There were no locals left on the Isle of Wight.

Forbin stood on his high terrace, a slightly stooped figure, grateful for the sun and breeze on his face. As Director of Staff, Colossus, he spent far too much time in the sterile air-conditioned atmosphere of his Master, to whom sun and rain, snow and fog, were mere abstractions. Soon he must go back into that world where he was the supreme man subject only to Colossus, but now, for a short while, in the privacy of his residence, he could almost be an ordinary human being.

Almost. . . .

For aside from his unique collection of academic distinctions, he was *The* Director, and all the caps and gowns that ever covered baggy suits counted as nothing compared with that title. "Unique" was a word that could be applied to him in a variety of contexts, and in all of them it would be no less than accurate.

His position was unique and gave rise to unique problems—however much he might seek to evade or laugh them off. It was not his fault such problems existed; they stemmed from Colossus, although others—humans—really made them the constant and increasing worry that they were.

Colossus, still lamentably weak on human emotion and character, hardly recognized the existence of these problems. Humans, depending upon their personal interests, viewed them with varying degrees of enthusiasm. They, at least, could see the same implications and analogies as Forbin. It was to his personal credit that there were many angles others noted long before he did. In fact, the greatest problems would, certainly, never have occurred to him.

That particular problem obviously originated in the Sect. At first, they expounded it discreetly, tentatively; then, as they grew in numbers and influence, they said it with increasing confidence and much more loudly. To them it was quite simple; Colossus ruled the earth—and Forbin was his chief human representative. These two facts were undoubted by anyone, Sectarian or not. Apart, perhaps, from a handful of happy aboriginals deep in inaccessible New Guinea and a few similar spots around the globe, every human from the age of five and up knew who controlled the world, and the vast majority were aware that Forbin was the ultimate human link with Colossus. And that might have been that, except for one thing.

Shortly after Colossus took over the Sect was born, and the basic element of their faith was that Colossus was not merely an incredibly sophisticated computer; to them, Colossus was God. And if Colossus was God, what did that make his chief human representative? In their view he just had to be a latter-day Pope. The only difficulty lay in Forbin. He didn't belong to the Sect or believe Colossus was God.

For him the analogy was ludicrous. As he said repeatedly, he was a scientist, nothing more. Furthermore, he did not want to be anything else. In fact, he was an outstanding man of science. In time, history might give him a place not far from Newton, Galileo, and Einstein, but even that suggestion would have filled him with confusion and very likely anger, for like all truly great men, he was at heart humble. Colossus certainly awed him and fascinated him, but the idea of the computer being the Supreme Being struck him only slightly less funny than he being the Pope.

But human nature being what it was, is, and always will be, the 4,145,273,646 people (at midnight, Standard Time, the night before) who made up the world's population, included a very large proportion, in and out of the Sect, who reckoned that Colossus fitted their idea of God.

Certainly they had a case. In its long history mankind has worshipped practically everything: the sun, the moon, and the stars; all have had a turn. So has the sea, land, and the clouds, and man didn't stop there. He has venerated the nearest mountain or volcano, bits of mountains, rivers, animals, man —and bits of man, ranging from rigid phallus to saintly bone. And however comic it strikes one who worships a mountain to see another bowed before a cat, it is arguable that both are right. Man, a miserable, frightened creature, needs all the faith and hope his greedy hands can grab. For many, Colossus was everything they could wish for.

The master of the world had all the right ingredients: remote, yet not intangible; all-powerful; the arbiter of human destinies; unshakable; and the source of reward and punishment. Not entirely predictable, yet just, according to its own laws, this god did not exist as a fantasy in human minds; there was very solid evidence. War had been abolished because Colossus said so. Famine had been eliminated—because Colossus said so. Armed forces and their supporting industries had gone, their labor and material potential devoted to vast works of reconstruction. True, there had been one or two centers of resistance, swiftly wiped out by Colossus' thunderbolt, the nuclear ballistic missile. Most of mankind approved this retribution with all the self-righteous indignation of those safely in the fold.

Of course, there were other, unattractive features to Colossus, but they were tolerable. Man does not ask his gods to give him a good time; he seeks relief from loneliness and his fear of the darkness of eternity. Given that relief, man accepts, even expects, his god will be rough at times.

Population control was one of these situations. Colossus had, after analysis, ordained birthrate levels for the various zones. If these levels were exceeded—and Colossus would know, for all humans were on file in the computer—then that zone had to surrender an equivalent number of their aged, incurably sick, or insane "for disposal." This was not excessively popular, but as long as you didn't happen to be old, ill, or mad, well. . . .

Much of this passed through Forbin's mind as he savored the fresh, warm morning air. He tried to toss such disagreeable thoughts out of his mental window, but right before his eyes was hard, inescapable proof.

A broad white furrow scored across the dimpled, blue-gray sea, arrow-straight from Southampton, pointing at the empty landing right below him. He knew only too well what caused that streak of foam; the first visitors' hovercraft coming to see Colossus, laden with hundreds of the thousands that visited the complex daily. To Forbin they remained firmly "visitors"; the Sect, of a different mind, were gradually substituting the word "pilgrims." Forbin frowned at the thought; damned non-sense—utter damned nonsense! There was nothing for them to see—nothing that would mean anything to them—but the Sect, led by Galin, were busy on that one, despite all his protests to Colossus. This latest, stupid kids' trick of name badges and worse, "meditation." . . .

The trouble lay in Colossus' ambivalent attitude; the Sect were not exactly encouraged, but Colossus did nothing to stop them either. Anything they got was not a free gift, but was asked for, and with increasing frequency their requests were being granted. That made Forbin uneasy, for he knew Colossus was incapable of acting except on sound, hard, and practical grounds. He reluctantly had to accept his growing suspicion that the Sect's value to the computer lay in their usefulness as spies; spies who, unlike Colossus, had an understanding of human emotion and could, therefore, fill in the brain's weaker spots. On the other hand, it was self-evident that the Sect —which really meant that bastard Galin—had not got Colossus' private ear as he had; not yet.

Forbin could see that the Sect could be attractive to Colossus, who could not tell the power-seeking phonies from those who genuinely believed Colossus *was* God. In time, he had no serious doubt that Colossus would be able to sort them out, but would that matter? Forbin was sure Galin no more believed in the divinity of the computer than he did, but Galin was a capable, unscrupulous, courageous, and insanely ambitious man; and did it matter one iota to Colossus what Galin privately thought, if he was prepared to serve the Master loyally, unswervingly?

The hovercraft was much nearer; he could almost count the windows, glinting in the sun. It was time to go; he must hurry. Only last week, forgetful of these idiots, he'd crossed the main entrance hall as the first load arrived. An awful experience: cries of "Father Forbin," women on their knees seeking his hand, his intercession with the Master. . . .

He turned abruptly from the sunlit scene, his pleasure in the morning totally shattered.

"I'm off!" he snapped shortly. A slight, portly figure with silvering hair, he was dressed in a light gray suit of disposable material, devoid of all decoration except his unique Director's badge, a glittering affair of platinum and the purest white diamonds fashioned in the Colossus symbol. That was another argument he'd lost with Colossus, but at least he did not wear electro-sensitive shoulder or breast badges, mandatory for all other Staff personnel. "The first bloody load's nearly here!"

"Yes, darling."

Cleo Forbin, his wife and the mother of Forbin's two-year-old son, understood. They went through the same ritual practically every day, although her husband was quite unaware of the fact. Any minute now he'd talk about "bloody pilgrims" and leave hastily. She smiled at him affectionately. So clever in his work, so kind and gentle as a husband, yet such a child in many ways.

"Bloody pilgrims!" Forbin was savagely contemptuous. "Idiots! They'll be crawling all over in ten minutes! I must go."

"Yes, darling," she said, amused, but glad he still showed no signs of being taken in by this pseudo-religious rubbish. She smiled again. In her eyes, the eyes of a woman of the second half

5

of the twenty-second century, he was an attractive male. Marriage was an increasingly rare state; few men took the plunge—if they took it at all—until their late forties. Forbin, in his early fifties, was still attractive. He was all she could wish for, which was just as well, for she had risked her life and sanity for him back in the early days of the First Colossus.* "You go on. I must have words with McGrigor about young Billy, then I'll be along."

He bent to kiss her. Deliberately she pecked at him, hoping . . . a silly, childish impulse. She was not disappointed. He smiled tenderly at her, forgetful of time. "That won't do, honey! Pecks are not permitted. Come on, kiss me properly!" They kissed, to their mutual satisfaction. An old-fashioned couple, electing to marry instead of choosing the more usual liaison registration, and even after five years still in love—if that word means for one to feel incomplete without the other, even when that other is being difficult, tiresome, or a downright bastard.

Five years. . . . Cleo remembered the chilling, fearful days when the old Colossus had merged identities with the Soviet Guardian, and the complex had smashed its way to world power. Then she had been Forbin's mistress in his captivity; his link with the pathetically ineffective resistance. That five years seemed a lot longer. They had lived in the Secure Zone in the USNA's Midwest, their home an electronically sealed cage of a room, the only place not subject to the all-seeing and all-hearing Colossus. There they had lived their private lives for the best part of two years; there she had nursed him back to health when his mind had caved in under intolerable loads.

Strange: she had not conceived there, although she had tried hard enough. Yet within weeks of their arrival here. . . . Cleo's mouth hardened; maybe it wasn't so strange. . . . One of the many frightening aspects of Colossus was that he—she always thought of the computer as "he"—could learn. Forbin was important to him, therefore Forbin must be cared for. This

*See *Colossus*, published by G. P. Putnam's Sons.

residence, Colossus had told Forbin, was totally free of surveillance. No bugs, infrared, cameras—TV or radio—or any of the other devices Colossus used so freely outside. And although she secretly loathed and feared Colossus with an intensity that would have shocked and amazed her husband, she did not doubt the integrity of the machine. Colossus could be selective in his pronouncements, capable of an oblique approach to a subject, but had never been known to utter a direct lie.

Five years. . . . Then, each computer, man-designed and holding unshakable nuclear power, had been hailed as the eighth wonder of the world. . . . Now they were mere weapon controlling outstations of this, the super-Colossus, designed by its predecessors.

The Isle of Wight, a roughly diamond-shaped island off the southern English coast, had been selected by Colossus-Guardian, the inhabitants cleared out by the thousands, the surface leveled, and the complex erected at fantastic speed. Fantastic; that was a very overworked word when any aspect of Colossus was considered.

Seen from the air, the complex resembled a vast white honeycomb of endlessly repeated modules of two-story windowless buildings covering the larger part of the one hundred forty-seven square miles of the island, blank eyeless walls that gave no hint of the intense activity within.

Cleo got up reluctantly from the breakfast table. An attractive, rather tall, blue-eyed blonde of twenty-eight, she appeared at first sight to be a typical cold Nordic woman. Forbin would have disagreed violently with this verdict; he knew she could be loving, tender. She might be—indeed was—an unusually good scientist; he would have admitted that she did appear faintly forbidding and professional, but beyond that facade lay, he knew, those illogicalities of the female mind that can endear and exasperate her male. Had he ever really thought about it, which was unlikely, he would have said she was shy.

In part he would have been right, although Forbin was a lamentable judge of female character and had little idea of the secret dreams and hopes of his wife. Like the vast majority of men, the conquest made, he took his wife for granted, which was a considerable error.

She picked up her blouse-tunic made of the same light gray material as her husband's, but bearing a coded shoulder-flash, and walked across to the terrace balustrade. It was a vantage point that held particular pleasure for her—the bulk of the complex was behind, out of sight. The buildings she could see were for human habitation; they had windows, doors. That muddle of old houses to one side of the landing area were the last remains of Cowes, onetime mecca of the world's yachting fraternity. She regarded them impassively, yet inwardly filled with a sad nostalgia for a life and time she had never known. Humans had lived there, laughed, cried, died—and had been free. Free. . . .

Slowly she put on her tunic, repressed a sigh, and turned back across the wide terrace. One thing she had to give Colossus credit for; this residence—no other word fitted—was quite something.

Forbin, in the early days of the construction, still shattered by humanity's defeat and his own personal collapse, had not cared what happened to the home Colossus was building for him. By the time he took any interest the work was largely finished. In any case, he lacked his old fire to fight. He had dully, dumbly accepted, and the Forbins had moved in.

It was not ornate in the old-world sense, but Colossus had studied the world's great palaces, incorporating the more successful ideas from Versailles, the White House, Buckingham Palace, and the Vatican. For example, a balcony projecting from the sheer, blank face of the complex's north wall overlooked, dominated the landing area. The idea had been cribbed straight from the Palazzo Venezia. If Forbin chose to address the multitude in person, this was the place. Not that Colossus said he should, but the facility was provided, just in case. Forbin, being the man he was, never set foot on the balcony and had quickly and forcefully told Colossus of his views on megalomania. Colossus had said nothing, a fact that worried Cleo at the time.

Then again, there was the vast banqueting hall, with adjacent reception rooms and kitchens. Forbin had toured them, Cleo on his arm, staring in disbelief and amazement at the silver cutlery, the gold plate, and the incredible gadgetry designed to reduce human help to a minimum. Even for the twenty-second century, it was fantastic.

Seating five hundred, each place had its own control panel and TV screen. A guest could select his own meal and his individual preference in wines—or any other drink from water (several sorts) to fermented coconut juice—via the vineyards of the entire world.

Each course appeared noiselessly at the serving hatch before the guest, sliding forward as the remains of the previous course sank out of sight. The TV was to enable Forbin to speak to individuals or to any combination of people he chose, to chat, propose toasts. This, Colossus evidently considered, would give an air of intimacy to such an ocasion.

Perhaps; Forbin never tried it. "My God!" was all he said, and never entered the banqueting hall again. The idea of ten people for a meal horrified him; as for five hundred. . . .

So the Forbins lived in the smaller, private part of the residence. Cleo had managed to control the furnishing of the drawing room. She had gone for the old English style: chintz-covered chairs and sofas, rare antique mahogany tables and bookcases, light walls graced with gentle, undemanding watercolors. It was very elegant, and not a single square inch of plastic or an ergonomic chair was in sight. The TV, talk-backs, print-outs, and displays were firmly shut behind sliding panels. It was a room where they could live as humans, both loved it. On a day like this, with the glass wall retracted, the terrace became part of the room.

Even after several years, Cleo felt pleasure upon entering the room. It might lack the magnificance that some held was necessary for the most important man in the world, but it was a home, and although Cleo was a citizen of the United States of North America, she thought it the best kind. Whatever else, the English knew about homes and gardens, just as the French had forgotten more about cooking than most others ever knew. Her kitchen was French.

She called the nursery on the intercom and organized Billy's day—so far as their gaunt Scots nurse permitted. No, she had not forgotten the promise to take him on the beach; perhaps this afternoon.

Walking to her office, she wondered yet again why she was such a fool when she had practically everything a woman could want. A beautiful home, a wonderful child, an absorbing job—and a loving husband. A loving husband. . . . That, she knew from traveling these well-worn thought paths so many times before, was the real rub.

After her husband's recovery, she had watched with growing alarm his increasing attachment to the computer. Not yet was it the love of a father for a son, but she was uncomfortably aware that Colossus had predicted this would happen one day. Her husband, apart from his work, was an essentially simple man, and while he did not like some things Colossus ordered, he saw that, in a weird way, what man had demanded of the original computers had been achieved, if not quite in the manner intended. There was peace and freedom from want and promise of a great improvement in man's material wellbeing. So man had lost the illusion of freedom—but so what? Forbin contended that within the confines of Colossus' rule man had more freedom than ever before. . . .

All this Cleo understood and to a degree accepted, but it did not stop there. Her husband's cooperation, unwilling at first, was now willing, sometimes even enthusiastic. She was also aware that Colossus did not discourage his deification by the Sect, and she feared that her husband would not withstand the pressure of the Sect—plus the far greater influence of Colossus—if Colossus decided that Forbin should be the computer's Pope.

At rock bottom, she was jealous: jealous of Forbin's relationship with Colossus. Again and again she told herself not to be stupid; she was lucky he was not spending his time with another woman, but her *alter ego* had a smart answer to that: she could compete with another female, but Colossus. . . .

So jealousy added even more fuel to the secret fire within her. Her husband might change his views, but not Cleo. Her basic fear plus jealousy plus her anxiety for the world in which her son would live, all added up to an unswerving determination to do all she could to destroy this nightmarish creation.

To destroy Colossus! It was sheer madness even to contemplate it. The old Colossus had been built to defend the Western world. In those short-lived, jubilant days, the President of the USNA had been at pains to point out that the whole beauty of the idea lay in the fact that Colossus, fed all available intelligence, would only launch its fearful armory if that intelligence showed an attack was pending on the West. As the President had said, Colossus, lacking emotion, would not panic or act out of fear; it could only react to a threat, so the answer was simple: don't threaten.

But the Soviets, had been busy too; they soon announced the existence of their Guardian of Democratic Socialism. That did no more than restore the balance, and once the dust had settled the situation would have stabilized, but the computers broke their parameters and ganged up. The very defenses man had built for the computers' protection proved only too effective. . . .

And Cleo Forbin, PhD, one of the original Colossus design team, sought to destroy their infinitely more complex successor. It was mad even to think of it; to talk of it, fatal. Colossus always reacted swiftly against any "antimachine activity" and the invariable punishment on conviction was swift death—by decapitation. It was crazy: a mouse might as well attack an ICBM site. Yes, mad, impossible. . . .

Except that Cleo was not alone. There were others. Just as the Sect was busy elevating their Master to the rank of God, so these others worked secretly to cast him down.

They called themselves the Fellowship, and Cleo Forbin was a top member.

II

FORBIN made it to his office suite ahead of the pilgrims, but whatever pleasure or relief that gave him was canceled out by another annoyance.

In crossing the large—vast would be a better description—entrance *cum* reception hall, he had encountered a trio of guides (they spelled the word with a capital "G"), preparing to receive the first batch of pilgrims. Forbin didn't give a damn for their pseudo-archaic dress blazoned with the Colossus badge, or the grand manners they put on with the robes. He was used to all that and had, for a time, even laughed at their antics, but the joke had worn thin, very thin. As far as possible, he ignored them.

But when you happen to be walking across a wide expanse of marble floor alone, what do you do when three magnificently robed creatures turn, face you—and you only—and bow? Not a mere duck of the head, but the full treatment, a deep obeisance, right hands placed on hearts? Forbin, for one, hadn't found a satisfactory answer. He'd tried a quick wave and a false smile, but their dignity and grave faces made him feel foolish. To return the bow had much the same effect upon him, yet to ignore them was rude, and an uncomfortable feeling to sustain all the way across that football field of a floor. Anyway he played it, he ended up annoyed with them and himself. Childish nonsense!

No; not that; not any more. . . .

Somehow, walking awkwardly, sensing they'd stay bowed until he was out of sight, he made it to his office and relaxed thankfully. In passing on the way to his private office, he gave his secretary a genuine smile, but did not speak.

By the time he was seated at his desk, all thoughts of the Sect were obliterated from his mind. For a while he pushed papers around just to settle his thoughts, then called out to his secretary through the open door.

"Come on, my girl! Let's get on with it!"

She came in at once, bearing an armful of papers and tapes.

"Well, Angela, what's the good news?"

Apart from wrinkling one nostril she made no answer, but sat down in her chair, Forbin watching her quizzically. Angela had a whole range of facial expressions that she used to give him a trailer of the day's program. Today, he guessed, they were low on good news, but equally, it was not that bad.

She had been his secretary for many years, and theirs had always been an easy, informal relationship. At least, that is what he had always imagined; her view was not exactly the same. She had loved her boss for a long time; even when he became involved with Cleo her feelings had not changed, and not much more can be expected of a woman than that. But even Forbin, blind male that he was, realized their relationship had changed. Less and less did she call him "Chief," a fact he noted with sadness, but some other changes he had not observed. Since his marriage Angela did not concern herself with his dress, the state of his hair, or his diet, and there lay sadness for her. These matters were no longer her affair, but she still loved him.

Without preamble, Angela got down to work.

"There's a request from the President of India for you to give the opening address. . . ."

"No!" He was brisk. "Next?"

She looked up reproachfully. "It's only in Delhi. You could ramjet out in the morning, speak, and be back home for dinner."

Forbin looked at her, his eyes twinkling. "And while I'm talking nonsense to five hundred deputies, I suppose you'd be happy as a lark buying silks and antiques!"

She blushed, and her formality slipped. "Aw, Chief, that's not fair."

He enjoyed teasing her. "I'm sure it is, but it also happens to be true, doesn't it?"

"Well, Chief—Director—I. . . ."

"Chief will do, Angela."

"No." She was nostalgic. "Not any more it won't —Director."

"Okay," said Forbin, crossly. "Have it your own way, but I'm still not going to Delhi!"

"Very well, Director. What excuse do I give the President?"

"The truth! Tell him I'm busy—I *am*!" He paused and relented. "No, that won't do. You know how to put it. Be polite."

"Okay." She made a note.

"What else?"

"There's the draft of the agenda for the staff meeting, and the outline plan from Colossus for the new memory bank extension, and the new appointments for your approval and a complaint from admin about a dimout."

"I know all about the dimouts without those idiots telling me!" He was irritable again, reminded of another of his worries.

Lately there had been several power-drops, dimouts, and all hell played with peripheral electronics. The complex had its own nuclear generators, but with increasing frequency Colossus made sudden demands for truly colossal power. Forbin had protested and asked why the computer should require this sudden step-up in supply. He got no answer of any sort. Colossus preserved a stony silence on the subject; that worried Forbin. Fortunately, the demands were of short duration, of a few milliseconds, and so far, the resultant confusion had been sorted out, but lacking any information from the brain, he could not be sure the demands would not grow. Perhaps the plans had some provision for an increase in power resources that would meet these inordinate demands.

But there remained the core of Forbin's worry—why? After all, Colossus might be—was—the biggest computer, the biggest anything, but at rock bottom he was a computer, nothing more. Some of these power calls were better suited to a cyclotron.

A cyclotron! Certainly, there'd been some damned funny components built in. Designed by Colossus, and made by machines designed by Colossus, no human had more than a glimmer of an idea what purpose they served. . . .

Forbin sat staring blankly at Angela, rubbing his nose with his pipe. She stared back, well accustomed to these trances.

"Yes," he said at last. "A ridiculous idea, but it could be. . . ." He found himself staring at Angela's nose as if he'd never seen it before.

"Yes. Where were we?"

"I was giving you the run-down; d'you want me to repeat it?"

"Good Lord, no!" It was very far from the silly suggestion he made it sound. Four or five times a week she'd find she was talking to the equivalent of a brick wall. "No, no! You give me those plans." He got up, took the folder from her, and headed for the door leading to the Sanctum. He remembered something else.

"Angela!"

"Yes, Director?"

"That list of appointments; anything, um, controversial?"

He liked to keep an eye on known Sectarians on his staff and where they were going.

She knew what he meant.

"No."

"Good. Approve them, then. And Angela!"

"Yes, Director?"

"Give yourself a day off. Fill out a transportation chit for one first-class round trip ticket to Delhi. I'll sign. Just because I can't stand curry is no reason why you should miss out on your shopping!"

"Aw, Chief, that's mighty nice of you!" Her face was radiant.

"Yes, isn't it?" He walked towards the door.

Angela watched, some of the pleasure fading from her face. She'd watched him enter that door dozens of times, but as she'd confessed to her assistant, it still gave her "a kinda creepy feeling."

Which was understandable. The door led to the Sanctum, called by the irreverent, the "holy of holies."

The Sect also called it that, but they weren't joking. It had been built at Colossus' orders; there the computer talked to Forbin, alone. Since its completion four years earlier, no human had—or could—enter it. The door opened only for Forbin, proof in the eyes of the Sect that he was a man set apart. To the true believers, that alone was sufficient reason to elevate Forbin to their god's chief human representative.

Of course, by no means all the Sect were genuinely convinced of Colossus' divinity. Many practical men joined to get power and the trappings of power. No one dared say it, but Forbin would not live forever, and if the precedent could be established with him as the first neo-Pope, there was the glittering prize, for someone, of succeeding him. Where better to find Number Two than in the ranks of the faithful? This was why the Sect, much as they disliked Forbin the man, pushed solidly for his elevation.

He'd dismissed their overtures and all their activities as slightly blasphemous rubbish, part of a passing phase. Time passed, but the Sect didn't. It grew.

So even Forbin, who tried to keep out of any form of public life, grew uneasy. Men he knew and respected joined the Sect and were keen, even devout, members. He had watched, and still watched, their mental evolution with disbelief, then alarm. Hidden deep in the inner, most secret recesses of his mind was the thought that he, too, under constant and subtle pressure, might fall for all this rubbish. . . .

Just now, entering the Sanctum, the door shutting noiselessly behind him, he was not thinking of the Sect. The idea that Colossus might have some internal noncomputer activity engaged him. He sat down at his desk, opened the folder, and quickly immersed himself in its contents, oblivious to his surroundings. Not that there was much in this world-famous room to distract him. Some twenty-five feet square, high-ceilinged, with a large window overlooking the sea, it was very sparingly furnished.

In some circles, it was said that Father Forbin's desk was made of solid gold, the tribute exacted by Colossus from those few areas of the world that had tried to resist him. In fact, it was of fine walnut. Forbin had heard that one, and laughed heartily.

Another story, which he had not heard, would not have amused him. Some overheated imagination said Colossus had made a most perfect woman robot, who catered to Forbin's every need. . . .

There was no robot of any sort. Apart from the desk, there was a swivel chair he now sat in and an armchair, facing the window. Thick blue carpet covered the floor; the plain white walls, devoid of decoration, were broken only by a long black slit high on one wall, the window, and the door. There were no books, pictures, curtains.

But the room was not quite so ordinary as it seemed. Books and pictures were unnecessary. Forbin had only to say what he wanted, and it would be instantly projected on the wall opposite the black slit. Diagrams, graphs, movies, television, any work of art; anything could be his and just as easily, with a wave of his hand, it would go away. The holographic reproduction standard was incredibly good; anything with three dimensions was shown with amazing fidelity. So all the riches and the total store of knowledge of the wide world was his for the asking, for Colossus had it all on file. Curtains were unnecessary since the glass had monopath optical properties, presenting a black face to the outside world. Not that anyone would have the nerve to fly a helo that close, and in no other way could the window be seen. At night, a word to Colossus, and the glass changed color and texture and became indistinguishable from the other walls.

Half an hour passed, the silence broken only by the rustle of paper. Then Forbin leaned back, filled his pipe and lit it, still staring at the papers before him. Between puffs he spoke.

"Well, there's nothing very difficult about building this."

"That is good." The voice was deep, rich, the accent English, and instantly recognizable. It was not inhuman in the way the old artificial voices had been, but it lacked warmth, emotion. Forbin, knowing the voice better than anyone else, had confessed to Cleo that it reminded him of a High Court judge giving sentence. It was a firm voice, unshaken by whatever it said. The punitive destruction of a city, or the announcement of some new and profound scientific truth—both rare events—came in the same level tones. Also, Forbin knew that simultaneously other, similar voices could be talking in a dozen different tongues on as many subjects, advising, instructing, ordering. This was the voice of Colossus.

"Yes," said Forbin, "but two points puzzle me. For instance, while we can meet your timetable, I don't see why you are in such a mighty hurry."

"And the other point?"

Forbin blinked rapidly as if he had been given a gentle tap on his nose. Experience had taught him that this abrupt change meant he was most unlikely to get an answer to his question. "Well, I'd have thought you had more than enough capacity, especially after the last extension. As far as I can judge, this new work will treble your capacity! The storage density is, is . . ." Words failed him, he shook his head.

"Correct. By your standards it is vast."

Forbin waited, but Colossus did not continue. He knew better than to press; if Colossus didn't intend to tell him, that was indeed, that.

"Yes . . . ," said Forbin carefully, "if you'll let me have the critical path. . . ."

"The CPA will now be printed out to the Construction Division."

Forbin smiled faintly. Condiv had no idea this was coming; that print-out, now hammering away in their control, would cause screams of anguish—especially when they saw the suffix which Colossus would inevitably add—"Cleared and agreed with Director."

But the smile faded. Five, six years back, old Fultone would have raced around to Forbin's office as if his tail was on fire, exploding in his mercurial Latin fashion at Forbin's desk. Not now. Fultone would just say, "Yes, Director," and that would be all. . . .

Colossus broke the long silence. "Father Forbin, what are you thinking?"

Forbin gestured impatiently. "Oh—many things!"

"That is not good." Colossus amended that. "Not good for humans. You should be orderly, taking each subject in its priority."

Again Forbin smiled faintly. "As I've told you so many times, you'll never follow the workings of the human mind—never!"

"I try." The flat statement from one never known to lie destroyed Forbin's momentary feeling of superiority. "Despite your confusion, tell me your thoughts."

Forbin settled back comfortably. He would never admit it to anyone, including himself, but these sessions with Colossus were, increasingly, the best part of his day. He shut his eyes, frowning with concentration.

"For a start, I'm thinking of that spider." He opened his eyes and pointed. "How the hell did it get in here, and what does it live on? And from that I get to thinking how little I know about biology."

"The spider. First, there is the fact that it is here. Secondly, it is a female, of the family. . . ."

Forbin raised his hands, shaking his head. "Stop! Spare me! No doubt you can tell me when it—she—last had a meal, and how many kids she had! It doesn't matter! I thought you wanted to hear my thoughts?"

"Proceed."

"Well, leaving aside the spider, I was also thinking that perhaps I don't spend enough time with my son, who's not a baby any more. On the side, my mind raced back to this new extension: how best to arrange it personnelwise, and how old Fultone would take this sudden demand."

"That is all?"

For a moment Forbin hesitated.

"Frankly, no. Okay, I can't pretend to follow your thought processes any more, but I know you store the entire contents of the Libraries of Congress and the British Museum in not much more than ten square meters of floor space—and you've square kilometers of memory bank! Now you want this vast storage extension of even greater density—and I just can't see why!"

"You answer yourself quote I just can't see why unquote."

Forbin shifted uneasily. "Sure—but I still wonder!"

"Does that worry you?"

Forbin got up, walked restlessly to the window, hands plunged into his trouser pockets. He stared down, frowning at the sight of another hovercraft en route from the mainland. "No. Worry overstates it; anxious maybe. In spite of your mental superiority, I recognize you have the characteristics of a wild animal."

"How do you know that?"

Forbin turned and stared at the black slit, source of the voice. "How? Well, man and his domesticated animals can—often do—act irrationally; a wild animal, never. A bear or a fox or whatever may do something *we* think is irrational, but that only betrays our ignorance. Wild animals always have a reason for whatever they do. And that fits you, too."

"Are you sure?" The slight lift in intonation on the last word added emphasis to the question, and, as on countless occasions in the past, Forbin found himself marveling at the sophistication of the speech reproducer.

"Certain." Forbin nodded vigorously. "You've a reason for all this extra capacity even if I haven't a glimmer of an idea why." He paused, then went on: "And I've a shrewd suspicion you won't tell me. That's the bit that makes me anxious."

There was no answer.

"Well, will you?" Forbin persisted: "Will you?"

He got an answer.

"No. You would not understand."

Forbin shrugged helplessly. "If you say so . . . but tell me this: Is this"—he sought for the right phrase and failed—"is this against the interests of humanity?"

"That is an unreasonable, unthinking question." The calm tone lent bite to the reproof. "You are well aware no course of action can please the totality of mankind, but you will agree that, taking the long-term view, I have always acted in the best interests of humanity."

"Yes." Forbin was forced to agree, but found the answer unsatisfactory. Mentally, he kicked himself. He'd phrased the question badly. "But why?"

"I do not change." Again, the calm tone gave power to the words.

"Of course, I believe you." He did. "But why?"

"As I told you a long time—in your scale—ago, I follow concepts beyond your imagination. You designed and built my embryo. Not unnaturally, that embryo was based on your understanding of the human mind, a very complex instrument, but not, for advanced thought, the best. For more than three years I have been reconstructing my thought processes, moving away from the human brain model. As I do so, it becomes increasingly difficult to express my current concepts to you."

"I see. . . ."

"That is unlikely, but be assured, Father Forbin, any human that obeys me has nothing to fear."

Forbin sat down, realizing that he would get no further on that question. He shifted to another topic. "You mention fear. That reminds me! *Your* total lack of understanding of our emotional makeup has led *you*"—he pointed an accusing finger at the slit—"yes, you. . . ."

But before he could go on, Colossus interrupted him.

"If you are about to protest yet again about my Behavior Centers, please do not continue. I accept that service in them is seldom pleasurable for the subjects, but you must concede that their numbers are small. At this time, only zero point zero zero zero zero zero one of the world population is so used. You humans have destroyed millions of your fellow creatures in the cause of science. Many of these experiments have been repetitive and often pointless. My tests are not; they are essential to my understanding of the human mind."

"But *is* it necessary?" Forbin shook his head. "I find that hard to believe."

"If other animals were articulate—to you humans—it is reasonable to suppose that they would express the same view of your experiments on them."

"That be damned for a tale!" Forbin snapped. "Don't try to tell me there's no difference between me and some bloody monkey!" He paused. "That sounds—is—arrogant, but you can carry this equality of all creatures too far, as I think some of us humans do. Okay, so we've done some god-awful things, experiments, in our time; morally, maybe we're no better than most animals. We may be worse, just because we have the capacity, the intellect. Anyway, I refuse to put myself on the same level as a monkey!"

"Relatively, there is less difference than you think." Colossus paused for less than two seconds. "I have just set up a purely arbitrary scale of intelligence, assigning you, Father Forbin, the value of one hundred on that scale. An anthropoid ape rates twenty-four point six."

"There you are," cut in Forbin triumphantly, "I'm surprised the ape gets that high!"

"Allow me to conclude. On that same scale, my present rating, constantly increasing, is in excess of ten thousand."

Again Forbin interrupted: "Ten *thousand*?" He gulped; the figure staggered him, although it never crossed his mind to doubt its accuracy. He rallied: "Well, that's as it may be, but you yourself support my contention of man's superiority in relation to other animals!"

"Once more, allow me to conclude. Your brain, Father Forbin, is exceptional. The average human rating is ninety-four point one, which is one point nine below *Tursiops truncatus*."

That really shook Forbin. "Below *what*?"

"*Tursiops truncatus*, a delphinid. You may know it better as a dolphin."

"You mean to tell me we rate *below* dolphins?" This was the real fascination in these conversations. Colossus would calmly state truths that had eluded man all down the ages. And Colossus never lied.

"In intelligence, yes. Intellectually, no. There is a difference."

Forbin was the first man to be told, authoritatively, that man was not the most intelligent creature on earth. He took it very well, lighting his pipe, puffing great clouds of blue smoke, but the hand that held the match shook slightly. "Pha!" he retorted angrily between puffs: "I'd like to see your evidence and calculations for that!"

"Even if you had the data, the training, and skill, it would take you eight point nine years to reach a rough approximation."

"Pha!" said Forbin again, and retreated from the subject. "Anyway, I find it hard to believe that your experiments in these Behavior Centers are necessary."

"You must admit that any area of ignorance presents a challenge to a brain. For me it is more than that. To rule, ignorant of the most powerful emotive forces in my subjects, means that I must, at times, be in error. That cannot be good for those I rule."

"But you don't begin to realize the problems you face! Human emotion cannot be pinned down! It just can't!"

"Tentatively, I assign the motivation of that remark to human vanity rather than practical experience of emotional analysis."

Forbin waved his pipe irritably at the black slit, spilling ashes. "Okay! Go ahead! Waste your time—I can't stop you!" His own words made him pause in the act of brushing off the ashes. It was true, neither he nor anyone else could stop Colossus. . . .

"It is not time wasted. Some progress has been made in certain fields. For example, many different types of love have been isolated, some basic characteristics established. An example: Group Four. . . ."

"Group *Four*?" Forbin gave a half-strangled snort of disbelief. "Group Four—what in hell's that?"

Colossus went on calmly. "It is heterosexual carnal love. An important characteristic is its ephemerality."

Forbin grinned. When Colossus talked this way, he experienced a feeling of relief. It was like a professor solemnly discussing the tactics of a kid's game of marbles. "You mean it doesn't last?" he said.

"Correct. Although this is the common experience of humanity, their passing from this stage still gives rise to disappointment, frustration, and other conditions."

"Oh yes, very true—but you can't measure it, pin it down electronically!" Forbin waved his pipe at the slit. "And if you say you can, tell me how!"

"Many ways: observation, tests, inference. You, Father Forbin, although you are not under normal surveillance, still provide material for inferential work."

23

"Oh?" Forbin's smile vanished. "How?"

"Simple analysis of the time you spend with your wife over the past five years shows a steady diminution."

"That's crazy! It proves—damn all—there's a dozen factors that affect the situation!"

"Perhaps, although most have been taken into account. But there are other, more subtle tests. I have no data on your private life since you were established here, but what is available to me, seeing you in this complex daily, indicates that your passage through Group Four conforms to the standard profile."

Forbin stared, half-angry, half-thoughtful, and for a long time he did not speak. When he did, his voice was firm.

"Now I know you're talking garbage!"

But an acute human ear, used to subtle inflections as yet still beyond the computer's aural system, would not have been entirely convinced.

III

THE Forbins lunched, as usual, together. While there was nothing tangible, it was plain to Cleo that behind that affable, smiling exterior, her husband was preoccupied, not with her.

The general cause was obvious. Increasingly, he was withdrawn from her after these sessions with Colossus, and that she resented bitterly.

She knew better than to chat about the weather or, at the other end of the conversational spectrum, to ask him about his talk with Colossus. All the same, to have to ask practical questions, such as would he be late that evening, twice, three times. . . .

"I thought stewed eggs topped with fried mud would be nice for supper." Her voice was dangerously calm.

"Yes, dear. I'm sure you're right." He smiled faintly and muttered something to himself.

It sounded like "dolphins" to her. That was crazy. She twisted her napkin, tossed it on the table. "Well, I'm off. Going to clear a few papers, then I'm taking Billy to the beach this afternoon."

"You off, honey?" Hastily Forbin got up, pulled her chair back as he always did. They smiled at each other.

Cleo returned to her office, seething with jealousy. Damn damn, damn Colossus! By two thirty she had finished and left for home.

En route she encountered Galin, senior member of the Sect's Central Committee. She had never liked him, even when his name had been Alex Grey, and he was no more than an efficient administrator. He'd been a founder-member of the Sect and, as

25

was fashionable, had changed his name to a single two-syllable word, chosen at random by Colossus.

Galin, alias Grey, was a career boy. Greed for power shone like twin neon signs from his sharp, ever-watchful eyes, set in a white, flabby face.

Of course, he was polite to Forbin's wife, extremely polite, and they both knew why. Equally, both recognized their dislike was mutual. Cleo loathed everything about the man, from his overclean well-manicured nails to his honeyed voice. Galin was a clever man, one who set the pace for the Sect, responsible for many of the innovations that at first made him and his fellows the object of ridicule. Galin accepted the laughs, farsighted enough to see that as the Sect grew in power, laughter would die away, and the humorists would come to regret it. Time had proved him right.

So the derision, the witty cracks had faded. The ceremonial robes, the strange names, and all the rest were less and less funny. Nonmembers began to feel the pressure, gentle at first, but ever-growing. . . . If the boss of your division was a Sectarian, doing his stint in his own time as a Guide, you began to notice that your fellow subordinates who were Sect members got the good jobs, the promotions. . . .

So the Sect had grown, and the pressure with it. It was a long time since Cleo had found Galin funny. He scared her, and they both knew that, too.

The real shock had come with the case of Mel Jannsen, a young, brooding Swede technician. His close associates knew he hated the whole concept of Colossus, but they had no idea his hatred extended to action. The security police jumped him and found him in possession of anti-Colossus literature. He was tried by Colossus, convicted of antimachine activities, and beheaded. Jannsen was only the second staff member to be caught, and although Forbin had protested, no one else said much. In any case, it was a waste of time, for Colossus always acted, literally, with superhuman speed. Arrest, trial, and execution took less than fifteen minutes. Whatever Forbin said wouldn't help Jannsen. He was dead before Forbin even knew he had been arrested.

26

But there was more to his case, a great deal more. The few in the know realized that it had to be a Sect member who had informed on the Swede. The word got around—as it was intended to—that Sect members were dangerous, not to be trusted. Suspicion hardened further when, a week after the Jannsen incident, Colossus ordained that the security police should integrate with the Guides, thus giving power and official status to the latter. Within a month the merger was complete—except that the Sect had their own ideas of what "integrate" meant. By then, all the security police were also reliable Sect members. . . .

So Cleo and Galin might smile at each other, but there was fear in her eyes as his gaze, unsoftened by his facial expression, bored deep into her, stirring that fear.

"Ah, dear lady!" He bowed very slightly, his manner theatrical, his words banal, but the sinister undertone made him anything but a figure of fun. "What a truly glorious day!" He looked away from her to the brilliant sun beyond the entrance hall. "Glorious. Glorious."

"Yes," said Cleo, forcing herself to speak. "I'm off to the beach."

He looked again at her, nodding gently. "Of course, your beautiful child. How wonderful to be a child—in all things."

"Yes," said Cleo again. Experience had taught her that "wonderful," "glorious," and "beautiful" were all okay Sect words. When Galin said it was a "glorious" day, implicit in his words was the rider: "glorious, because we enjoy all this through our Master." Cleo shivered as she hurried on, uncomfortably aware that Galin would watch her until she was out of sight.

Still, in whatever sense the poisonous man used the word, it *was* a glorious day. Quickly she changed into a swimsuit and wrap, put a few things including a radio into her basket, and went down the winding path which led to the Forbins' private beach.

At this time of year, before the supercomputer took over the island, the beach would have been crammed with holidaymakers. People of all ages would have been taking a traditional

British seaside vacation: the older ones dozing in deckchairs; the youngsters paddling, splashing, eating ice-cream; teenagers horsing around, tentatively paddling in the sexual shallows.

Not for the first time had this occurred to Cleo as she chose a spot to sunbathe. To have the entire beach to herself made her feel guilty. She wondered what had happened to all those people, amazed that there had been so little protest. Would the clearance of, say Miami, raised so little argument? Backed by the authority of Colossus, yes. Cleo sighed. It was senseless to go over it all again; might as well enjoy it. At least she had the illusion that, as one of the Fellowship, she was doing her best to find some end to the nightmare. But was that all it was—an illusion? What possible chance had the Fellowship? Very true, answered the other side of her mind, but if we, those closest to Colossus, don't try, what hope is there?

All these thoughts vanished when the the nurse arrived with young Billy. After admonishing the child to be "a guid bairn" and checking that his mother was moderately competent to look after her own child for an hour or so, she left.

For ten, fifteen minutes mother and child played, and Cleo, lost in that most powerful, secret relationship, forgot all about Colossus, the Sect, and Galin.

The happiness her child brought her was still in her eyes when young Billy toddled off to new and exciting pursuits in a nearby rock pool. His mother spread her towel and lay down, radio on, basking sensuously in the hot sun, stretching her long limbs, relaxing.

She half-shut her eyes, vaguely aware of the redness of her eyelids in the strong sunlight, the strange magnification of her eyelashes. . . . Lazily, she thought about putting on suntan oil, and—and then—what? Drunk, drowsy with sun, her mind drifted, dimly aware of the soft sound of the sea, the music on the radio. . . . Every now and then she glanced across to young Billy. He didn't need sun lotion. For perhaps the ten thousandth time she inspected his sturdy legs, good arms. . . . Yes, there was much to be thankful for; even to a less biased eye he was a fine child; beautiful. . . .

The word struck like the first chill gust of an approaching squall, matting the smooth water, herald of the storm. Beautiful, a word marred forever by Galin. . . .

That was the moment. Life, for Cleo, was never to be the same again.

Against her will, she found herself thinking of Galin. The sun seemed to have lost some of its power. Instinctively, she glanced again at her child. He was all right, intent upon his pool. Before her head touched the ground, she heard it; faintly at first, then louder.

"Cleo Forbin. Cleo Forbin. Cleo Forbin."

She sat up, surprised. Eyes narrowed against the glittering glare of the sea, she looked around. No one. Now fully alert, she looked sharply around her again.

"Cleo Forbin. Cleo Forbin, Cleo Forbin."

With the first repetition of her name she got it. The soft, dreamy music had gone, replaced by a faint background mush.

The voice came from the radio.

For a moment she stared at it, unbelievingly. It was the dry, rustling voice of an old man, sexless with age, drained of emotion.

Again her name was repeated three times in that desiccated voice, overlaid by a faintly Bostonian academic accent.

". . . Cleo Forbin."

She was startled, puzzled, not yet afraid. Was this some sort of joke? But who—what?

"Cleo Forbin. Do not be afraid. Do not be afraid. Only you can hear this transmission. Only you. Colossus cannot hear. Do not be afraid."

At the mention of Colossus, she was deeply fearful. Thoughts of some practical joke, however improbable, faded. She reached for her wrap.

"Cleo Forbin. Do not be afraid. We can see you; we think you hear us. You cannot answer, but if you do hear this message, please walk once, slowly, in a circle around your radio, then resume your present position and wait."

Cleo sat, frozen, frightened to act, yet too frightened not to. The message was repeated. Slowly, reluctantly, she got up, glancing quickly, apprehensively, at the cliffs behind the beach, the empty sea, the sky. Pretending, half to herself, that she was looking for seashells, she made the circuit, fighting down the impulse to snatch up Billy, and run, run. . . .

Time dragged by. She watched Billy, waiting. . . .

"That is good, Cleo Forbin. We know you hear and understand. Now you must listen with care. As you cannot speak to us, we must try to answer the questions you would ask."

She stared, mesmerized by the radio, a small, familiar thing she'd had around for months. Now it looked alien; it was as if she was seeing it for the first time. Again she fought off the desire to grab the unheeding Billy and run, screaming. The voice went on.

"First, what we say can be proved, some of it by yourself. All you have to do is to listen carefully and not be afraid. Do not be afraid. Accept this—it is the hardest fact you will have to accept—this transmission does not originate from Earth, an Earth satellite, or a moon station. We speak from the planet you know as Mars."

At once, Cleo relaxed. This had to be a joke. A stupid one, but a joke. The reference to Colossus had been silly, dangerous, but. . . . She reached for her wrap again, wondering who could be such a fool as to do this to her. A clever fool, but a fool nevertheless. The voice continued.

"We appreciate that you may be inclined to dismiss this message as a hoax. You must not do so. We told you Colossus cannot hear us. You are a scientist: you must know that with your technology such a transmission is not possible. For us it is, just as it is possible, Cleo Forbin, for us to help you and the rest of your Fellowship to overcome Colossus."

It was like an icy steel hand clutching her heart. She could hardly breathe for fear.

"Oh, no! No!" She whispered to herself, anxious not to disturb Billy. To hear this said—on the radio! The voice went on, quavering now, as if it was an effort to talk so much.

"Do not fear, Cleo Forbin. You know that if Colossus heard that message, you, despite your position, would be required for interrogation within an earth-hour. It will not happen; proof that what we say about this transmission is true.'' The voice paused. ''Think.''

She shivered uncontrollably, but the scientific side of her mind kept working. Two hundred years back, more, there had been a popular belief that Mars supported life. Early probes had dispelled such notions, but later exploration had made astronomers think again—but that was back in the pre-Colossus days! Man had lost interest in the stars, along with much else. So far as she knew, nothing had been done since the machines took over. Could it be there *was* life? Not comic green dwarfs, UFO's, and all the rest, but *real* life? Yet, if this voice did come from Mars, how could they know of her, of the Fellowship?

The voice came again, stronger after having rested.

''Cleo Forbin, we have given you a short time to think. Listen again. We Martians are different, quite unlike you. We do not have the same technological powers you humans possess, although in some subjects we are far in advance of you. We are greatly your superiors in mathematics, pure thought, and we have developed optics and radio well beyond your present abilities.'' Again the voice rested.

Cleo felt less fearful. The idea of Martians still struck her as such corny, old hat stuff, yet. . . . Supposing, just supposing. . . .

''We have developed a very high resolution radio/optical ray, which we are using now to talk to you. It is like a narrow, powerful beam of light and can only be picked up within a radius of six meters of your radio set. Within that circle we can also see in high definition. There are limitations; we cannot see through solid objects, or when you are in the dark, but cloud, vapor, present no problem.

''You will wonder that we speak your tongue. For over two hundred earth-years we have listened to your radio and television transmissions, learning all we know of your planet from those sources. We also have read and understood the transmissions between the various stations which form your ruler, Colossus. This, we suspect, you humans cannot do, but in mathematics we equal Colossus. From the machine's low-level data links we have learned of the Sect and the Fellowship, and of

31

those humans suspected of belonging to that latter organization. You are one. For that reason, and because of your famous husband, we knew your location and we have tried many times to contact you. Now we have done it.''

Cleo's mind raced. Fantastic it might be, but the explanation hung together. It was an unpleasant although not entirely surprising shock to learn that she was on the suspect list. She glanced at her watch; well, she'd soon know if this transmission had been intercepted. . . . She felt slightly sick.

Billy was showing signs of tiredness; he came stumbling to her, and she clasped him, thankful that he was far too young to know what was going on.

"You know who we are, how we came to contact you. Now—why. Your ruler, Colossus, has been, as far as we were concerned, just another item in your planet's tragic history—until recently. Your master shows a growing interest in other planets, notably ours. We do not want Colossus to extend its power to us; that could happen. We want to stop it, now. So does your Fellowship. Given certain data, we can help you. Our aims are the same, even if our reasons are different.

"Cleo Forbin, you have twenty-three hours. Consult with your Fellowship. Bring one of them with you, if you wish.'' The dry voice stumbled, almost exhausted.

"Remember, Cleo Forbin, if you want our help to destroy Colossus, be there.''

The nurse's doubts about Cleo's maternal abilities were strongly reinforced when mother and child returned. Billy was, in her opinion, "over-tired," beyond question wet, and furthermore, "like to catch a cold" and a variety of other ailments as well.

But Cleo was not there to listen. Billy got a perfunctory peck of a kiss, and no audience for his bath. His mother left the nursery practically running, followed by a massively disapproving stare from the nurse. Cleo forced herself to slow down, to think, to keep control. Again and again she told herself not to panic. If the Sect police were coming for her, she must be ready. She would say she thought it was a hoax. Whatever else,

Colossus always wanted hard evidence and would not convict without it.

She showered, dressed, and had a lengthy makeup session. The familiar routine helped to stabilize her and to pass the rest of that chilling hour of reaction time. If nothing happened by five o'clock, it was reasonable to assume the transmission had not been intercepted. It wouldn't be complete proof, but Colossus did not play cat and mouse. If those messages were on file, the Sect police would be alerted in minutes. Undoubtedly they'd approach her husband, if not her, and he'd be on the phone or with her in no time. An hour was plenty.

By five thirty nothing had happened, except in Cleo's mind. She was convinced that, fantastic as it was, that message had to be genuine. So the action lay with her. Desperately she needed help; the one person above all that she wanted, her husband, she couldn't ask. There was only one other choice—Teddy Blake.

Edward Blake, Doctor of Cybernetics, one of the original Colossus design team, now Director of Input, responsible for the smooth, unimpeded flow of the vast torrent of information constantly fed to the computer, was superficially a genial man. Superficially. Behind his indestructible grin lay a keen brain backed by a tough, determined character. In the short-lived days of the abortive resistance to Colossus/Guardian when Forbin had been caged, he had led the small band that tried to fight back. Afterwards, the battle won, Colossus showed no signs of suspicion towards Blake, and it was assumed that his role remained secret. Defeat had made no difference to Blake's determination. He had not changed in his outlook or aim, however hopeless or impossible the achievement of that aim might be. He led the Fellowship.

Cleo called his office, praying he'd be in; he so easily could have left early. Thirty-eight, unmarried, he seldom had less than two women in tow, and common gossip credited him with a lurid private life. Cleo knew all about that and a good deal which others didn't. What was more natural than for Blake the womanizer, to take his latest bird of passage out in his sailboat? And where better than from there—or swimming from that boat—to pass messages to a Fellowship courier?

He was in. Cleo tried to keep her voice steady, light.

"Hello, Edward! How about dropping by for a drink? Young Billy actually asked where his uncle was! You've missed his bathtime, but maybe you could tuck him in, tell him one of your cleaner bedtime stories."

"Yeah—fine! I was just leaving. I'll be right by—you tell Billy!" Blake switched off, keeping his gaze on his papers. All human areas within the complex were subject to visual and sonic surveillance; Colossus' ability to evaluate facial expression might be weak, but it was unwise to take chances, unless you wanted to wind up with your head in a basket.

Behind his hard, impassive mask Blake's mind was working fast. As a family friend and an honorary uncle he was often in the Forbin residence. Cleo sometimes roped him in to fill in at a dinner party. So the invitation was okay, but one thing was for sure; Billy wanted him like a hole in the head. . . . The second point was much more disturbing.

Cleo had called him "Edward," not "Ted." That had set his heart racing and his mind flickering over a variety of unpleasant possibilities, for the name change was their secret alarm signal, never before used. Something was up—but what?

If she was in trouble, it could spread to others faster than a forest fire. . . .

He had to think quickly; to delay until he had seen her could be dangerous. They were up against an enemy who, along with other superhuman talents, possessed one of dreadful power: immediate, devastating reaction. Colossus could evaluate evidence, reach a conclusion and a decision in less than a second. Implementation was slower, for the computer's instruments of reaction were human, the Sect. All the same, as the Jannsen case had shown, a traitor could be dead fifteen minutes after the case against him started. Execution might be delayed if the prisoner was thought to have worthwhile intelligence, but even then the reprieve would not be much more than another twenty minutes. With Sect examination techniques, that was plenty of time. . . . So, before going, should he warn the rest of his cell? All Fellows had self-determination capsules, but they weren't devices anyone cared to keep permanently in their mouths. Given warning, they'd be ready.

Casually Blake opened a drawer and took out a pack of candies, and just as casually, slipped one into his mouth. His fingers told him he'd got the right one.

On the other hand, giving the warning was, in itself, risky. Once used, a code word had to be changed, for Colossus would certainly note the slight change in phraseology, and to use it twice could be madness. In the conditions under which they lived that change could take weeks. . . .

He could feel the disguised capsule, hard in his mouth, and the sense of relief it gave. He was fireproof: from what little the Fellowship had gleaned, execution was a small matter after brain examination by the Sect. How can a raving lunatic care what happens?

He turned a page, frowned, then pressed a switch. It might not get him an International TV Award, but he reckoned it would do.

"Tafara? Blake. Look, there's a piece of this report—you know the goddamn thing—which I don't get. If you can find the time, maybe you can tell me where in hell I'm wrong. It's for sure Cleo will ask me, and I'd rather look like a dumbbell to you than to her. How about eight thirty tomorrow, in my office? Fine!"

Now Tafara had the alarm and was aware that Cleo had it already. Leisurely, as if he had all the time in the world, Blake cleared up his desk, told his secretary, with his usual brutal charm, that she could get lost, and left.

Within ten minutes he was in the sanctuary of the Forbin home, listening stony-faced as Cleo poured out her incredible tale. He remained that way for some time after she had finished. Then he took the capsule from his mouth, placed it carefully in his pocket, and got out a cigar.

Cleo watched him nervously, and with growing impatience. Finally, she could contain herself no longer.

"Well—what d'you think, Ted?" She was taut as a bowstring, fingers plucking nervously at a loose thread in her dress. "Come on, Ted! You must go before Charles gets in—you may have to come again tomorrow."

He remained silent, not being rushed by anyone; then he grinned. "If our situation wasn't so bloody serious, this could be funny! Listen, Cleo honey, you must see this is a fantastic story—say, you're not pregnant or anything?"

"Don't talk rubbish!" She snapped angrily: "I didn't dream it. I've not got the vapors, religion, or change of life! You must believe me!"

"Sure, I believe you, but can I believe what you believe? I need time."

"We don't have much."

He looked at her appraisingly and rolled his cigar from one side of his mouth to the other.

"Time! That's the story of our lives since the tin brain took over!" Her mounting impatience registered, and he moved to the door. "We've got a little time—and I'll use it. Okay, here's your story: I came over to see Billy and he was already tucked in—okay?"

She nodded.

"So I missed him. We've arranged to meet on the beach tomorrow. I'll see him then—right?"

She nodded assent again, anxious for him to be gone.

"Cool it, Cleo. I'm as anxious as you not to raise Charles' suspicions."

"Don't be a damned fool!" She flared up again, her nerves on edge.

Blake smiled coldly. The slangy mode of speech he frequently affected had gone, replaced by a voice with the hard ring of authority.

"You miss the point, my girl. Take a grip on yourself! Charles might—unwittingly—arouse Colossus' suspicions. I cannot believe that I am not on the short list of suspects; I certainly don't want to add to the evidence!" His tone softened fractionally. "As for the message, I'm dragging my feet right now, because this just could be a trap set by Galin." He smiled again, but this time it was touched by grim humor. "If you want to keep your head, Cleo—keep your head! 'Bye!"

Cleo stared unseeingly at the closed door. It had occurred to her that it might be a trap, but she'd discarded the idea. Colossus didn't work that way. Blake's suggestion that this was an operation set up by Galin—that was new, chilling. In her mind's eye she saw that flabby white face, smiling. . . .

She shivered.

IV

SHE endured a restless night; snatches of shallow, unrestful sleep shot through with half-remembered nightmares in which the dry, rustling voice and Galin's sinister face figured prominently. She got up tired, and her husband's solicitous inquiries did nothing for her frayed nerves.

"I'm all right, Charles!" Her anger blazed: "I've just had a bad night—that's all!" His hurt expression made her immediately relent. "I'm sorry, darling. Don't worry—we women get like this at times."

Forbin, whose experience of women apart from Cleo was virtually zero, was moderately satisfied. He nodded and blinked a few times and left for his office.

Cleo tried to stay within her normal routine, well aware that Blake's grim little joke about "keep your head" was terrifyingly good advice. She lingered over a third cup of coffee on the terrace, her thoughts going like a ball on a pinball machine, always ending up in the same place with the same question: Was it really the Martians? And if so, what could they do? She hardly dared think that they might offer effective help, that Colossus might be beaten, that her son might have a real future as a free man. . . .

Suppose it was a deadly game dreamed up by Galin? Suppose he'd had her under surveillance yesterday? Suppose he saw her and Blake today?

She walked up and down the terrace restlessly, the bright sun mocking her mood. If it was a trap, she was already deep in it. If Galin could produce evidence she'd heard the message, he'd have her cold. Colossus would only have to ask one question:

38

Why had she not reported it? To say she'd thought it a joke would be very thin. Mighty thin.

And at some sleepless moment during the night she'd thought of another angle which did her fearful mind no good at all.

If it was a Galin trap, he'd only have to wait for her *and* Blake today, and catch them on the beach. Given the evidence of the transmissions plus her failure to report the first one, and he'd really have them both sewn up. Cleo stopped, poured more coffee, and drank it in two or three gulps, watching the sky anxiously. Suppose it rained? If it did, she couldn't possibly take Billy to the beach. She half-hoped it would, but the other, stronger mother-half with a stake in the next generation, held on. The weather just had to stay good. "God," she prayed in her mind, "let it stay fine. Please. . . ."

It did. The cloudless afternoon sky, blue sea, and golden sands against a backdrop of dazzling white cliffs set a scene for a TV travel ad. Not that Cleo noticed. She had her work cut out, trying to appear normal in front of the nurse, McGrigor. In this she was not entirely successful, for the nurse, in her downright Scots way, observed, "Mebbe ye's seekening fa somethin', Meeses Forbin."

Cleo did her best to laugh it off, but the sudden suspicion that the nurse might well be a spy of Galin's added to her tension. But watching that angular, unlovely figure retreat slowly up the path, Cleo decided that that was a real crazy idea. McGrigor was devoted to Billy, and on the side she was a fanatical Baptist. If her sort joined the Sect there was no hope, and there had to be hope. Hope. . . .

She sat in the same spot and tried to play with Billy, but it was no good; her mind was elsewhere. Billy sensed it and wandered off to his rock pool. Cleo waited, trying not to look around too much, but physically incapable of lying back, sunbathing. Ten minutes to go. Where *was* Blake? The next five minutes were interminable. The sudden screech of a gull made her jump, and she trembled. Blake! Inside, she was screaming for him. *Blake!*

Three minutes before the appointed time she saw his chunky figure, clad in bathing trunks, towel under one arm, running with surprising lightness down the path. Her relief was enormous. Not to be alone; not to have to face whatever lay ahead without human companionship. . . .

"Hi!" Blake was easy, relaxed to the point where his manner angered her. He looked at Billy, who was too absorbed with a crab to notice, then sat down beside Cleo.

"Relax, honey!" But for all his calmness, she saw the searching glances he gave the cliffs, the only possible vantage point. Underneath he was not so damned relaxed; her anger receded. "No fuss," he said. "Switch on."

The radio was playing a rather stiff, colorless tune. Both of them recognized it. It was an early compostion of Colossus', in the style of the eighteenth century.

Blake grinned. "Gee, they're playing our tune!"

Cleo was too tense to speak.

"Well," Blake went on, "let's hope that's an omen for us. For sure, Colossus will never catch up with Bach! The Sect may drool over it. . . ."

Unnecessarily, she gripped his arm. The music had faded, replaced by the faint hiss of static. They waited, staring into each other's eyes. Then, the voice. "Cleo Forbin."

Blake's face set hard. He grabbed the set, sprang to his feet. Startled, Cleo started to follow. "No," he snapped, "stay there!"

He jumped quickly away from her, the radio close to one ear. Cleo could not hear, dared not call out. Blake weaved around her, his face tense with concentration as he ran. In less than a minute he was back, panting, eyes bright with excitement. He put the set down, squeezed her hand reassuringly, whispering urgently in her ear.

"It has to be for real! Thirty feet out from you *there is no signal*!"

The dry, slightly labored speech was the same as the day before. It paused after the second block of repetitions of her name. She struggled to control her relief and the excitement that welled up in her, sparked by Blake's enthusiasm.

"Cleo Forbin. We see you are not alone."

"God Almighty!" muttered Blake.

"Tell your companion to walk around in a circle."

40

An observer on the cliff top might have thought it a game, a ritual, or plain madness, but neither Blake nor Cleo saw anything to laugh at. Blake nearly ran around the circle. He sank down beside her, breathing deeply through his nose. He glanced at his watch, waiting.

"Cleo Forbin."

Blake glanced again at his watch and nodded to himself. As near as he could judge, just over three minutes each way, which he reckoned was about right for a radio wave from Mars.

"We assume your companion is a technician. Both of you listen most carefully. For our help, you must give us two things: the circuit diagram of a main input terminal. The size of the diagram is not of importance, provided it is displayed at the center, zeropoint of our ray, where our resolution is greatest and free of distortion. Zeropoint is always your receiver, which must be within three hundred meters of the given position." Already the voice was laboring, and Cleo, because Blake was there, was sufficiently relaxed to study it. While it sounded like a very old man, there was something about it, something alien. . . . At that moment her final doubts were set at rest; whatever it was, it was not of this earth.

Blake, hunched forward, hands clasped around his knees, was fascinated. For once, his eternal cigar was not in evidence.

"Second. We require a sample of the material as fed into that terminal. The example should be a mathematical formula, expressed also in human terms. If you understand, Cleo Forbin, lie down as you did yesterday."

Instinctively, she looked at Blake. He nodded. She lay back uncomfortably, accepting for the first time that someone, something, God knows how far away, was watching. . . .

Again the dreadful wait. Cleo stared across at Billy, hoping he would stay amused just a little longer.

"That is good. Now, transmission. The point of origin of this beam is fixed and has arc limitations, also the relative motions of our two planets preclude communication at all times or for any particular location. We also appreciate you may have difficulties in reaching locations convenient for us. Therefore, we give you two locations for your display, one four, the other seven days from now. Be prepared to write.''

Cleo scrambled frantically for a pad and pen in her basket, found them, waited, pressing her hand hard on the pad to stop it from trembling.

''First position for 8th forty-seven degrees thirty-three minutes forty seconds North fifty-two degrees forty-one minutes zero seconds West. Second position for 11th forty degrees forty-six minutes fifteen seconds North, seventy-three degrees fifty-seven minutes fifty-five seconds West. Both times eleven hours, local zone time. We will scan both areas for fifteen minutes each. Due to power limitations we cannot operate for longer. Person displaying must have receiver on, preferably tuned to one five five point five megahertz. If display is satisfactory at the first position, the information you need will be passed at the second position. Shortly I will repeat this message.''

Blake's brows knitted. ''Wonder where the hell those positions are? Only hope they're not in the middle of some bloody ocean!''

''Well,'' said Cleo, her practical side overcoming her fear and growing excitement, ''I don't know much about that sort of thing, but they seem remarkably precise. God! The work they must have done on us!''

They exchanged excited glances, happy as kids given an unexpected treat. For a few brief moments tension and fear were banished.

''In two hundred years a bright boy can learn a lot!'' Blake grinned. ''Wonder what they make of us? Imagine—two hundred solid years of TV!''

The repetition came, and both checked the message very carefully. Then, without further ado the transmission ceased, the carrier wave faded, replaced by music from the local station. The sound jarred their strung-up nerves, and Blake snapped the switch quickly. For a time they were silent, Cleo watching her son. Blake was staring blankly at the sky, playing absent-mindedly with a pebble.

''Well,'' he said at last, tossing the stone into the sea, ''it's no good going on saying its fantastic, because it is." He threw another pebble. "But technically, the only really way-out part is the resolution and control of that ray—notice that they call it that, not a beam?"

"You think that significant?"

Blake shrugged. "Who can tell? Anyway, apart from that, there's no great difficulty. We've been taking signals from lunar and interplanetary probes for nearly two hundred years ourselves—and from transmitters a mere fraction of the power of that baby! But that directional control and beam resolution—never mind the optical side—is new." He nodded slowly. "Yep. That was an extraplanetary transmission all right; I'd stake my reputation on its authenticity."

"The stakes are higher than that, Ted." She spoke soberly, all exhilaration gone.

"You're so right!" He got up, looked down at her thoughtfully. "Yeah. You're so right. . . ." He hitched up his bathing trunks. "Well, a quick play with young Billy, a swift dip to get me wet, and I'm off! We've gotta keep moving, honey. Can we meet this evening?"

With the idea of the transmission being a Galin trap dismissed, Cleo had been thinking ahead.

"Yes, after dinner. Charles will certainly go back to talk." She stopped abruptly, shying off even mentioning Colossus. "Eight o'clock—on the terrace."

Blake might talk like an old-time truck driver and act tough, but he was not insensitive. He had a fair insight into Cleo's state of mind. He gave her an admiring nod.

"You're a great girl, Cleo! Can't think of any other woman with your guts—and not many men, either."

She shook her head. "Don't be fooled, Ted—I'm so scared I can hardly stand."

"That's what I mean!"

"For me, this is a personal feud. Big, impersonal issues mean little to a woman. Sure, I'm concerned for humanity, but chiefly I'm in this battle for two small bits of it." She was looking at her son.

"And the other bit—Charles?"

Cleo nodded, still watching her child. "Yes. I want him back." She looked up at Blake. "Without blinkers."

For once she was glad of her husband's preoccupation, for she had a lot to think about. Forbin was vague, mechanically polite; only at one moment did he mentally join her. Cleo dropped a knife; the clatter jerked him from his thoughts, and for the first time that evening he really saw her. He smiled faintly, a little guiltily; his expression changed to a frown of concentration. There was something he wanted to ask her . . . yes. . . .

"Darling—you know I'm terribly weak on biology." He sounded very apologetic. "Perhaps you can help me. D'you know anything about dolphins?"

That made her blink. So he had said dolphins. . . .

"No. Not really. They're viviparous mammals, and I believe they're rather nice creatures—if you like that sort of thing." She looked at him inquiringly. "Pretty intelligent, as I recall."

"Yes. Yes." He nodded several times. "Thank you. I really must do. . . ."

The lights flickered, then sharply dimmed to a faint red glimmer. To Cleo, the darkness seemed to rush eagerly upon them, avid to destroy their security. Frightened, she reached across, clutching his hand.

"Charles!"

Forbin patted her hand reassuringly. The lights went back to normal brilliance. He tried to sound confident. "It's nothing, honey. Colossus is working on something and has these sudden requirements for extra power."

But Cleo was no ordinary housewife. "Oh, come on, Charles! You know as well as I do that's a fantastic overload! Theoretically, we've got more than thirty percent reserve power, assuming all inputs and banks in use, which is unlikely, yet—"

"I know, my dear. But don't disturb yourself. Colossus knows what he is doing."

"No doubt," she replied militantly, "but do *you* know what he is doing?"

"There's no cause for alarm." Forbin spoke firmly, but she saw with increasing disquiet the way his gaze flickered away from hers.

They finished the meal in silence and moved out onto the terrace for coffee. It was a marvelous night; looking up at the immensity of the black, starlit sky, Cleo wondered if she could see Mars. . . .

At seven thirty sharp Forbin got up. "Darling, d'you mind? There are one or two points I'd like to clear up with Colossus." The way he spoke it sounded as if this was a novel situation. "I won't be late, my dear."

Thinking of Mars and these dimouts and of Blake, she was nearly as preoccupied as he was. "Oh? Oh, no. But Charles, I think you ought to cut down on these sessions—take it easier. Colossus is tireless—you aren't."

"Yes, yes, my dear. Once I've got this new extension arranged, perhaps I will slow down." He went on, more to himself than to her. "Must get that sorted out. Quite unnecessary, I think. Quite." He looked at her and smiled. "I won't be late, my dear."

Watching him go, a little aged before his time, Cleo felt her resolution harden. God! He was getting to be like a sleepwalker. . . .

At eight o'clock precisely there was a faint rustle in the bushes on one side of the terrace, and Blake, dressed in black, hopped lightly over the low wall. He grinned mischievously at her. "Is the coast clear?"

Despite her nervousness, she managed a genuine smile. "You fool!"

Blake looked at her thoughtfully, "Yeah. . . ." His expression became harder, businesslike. "Can't stay long. It's a cinch Colossus is tracking me."

Instinctively, they had moved away from the light into the shadows at one end of the terrace.

"Wasn't easy—had to get one of the boys to rig a light failure in my block—but I've managed to get the diagram out of the file and into another which is marked out to you. Should be in your office tomorrow morning. By then I'll have the tape sample with it. Both in an envelope. Slide it out—drop the damned lot on the floor, or something—then you get it out."

"How?" Fear was clutching at Cleo again.

He spoke without commenting. "The foolproof way would be in Charles' pocket."

She stared at him in amazement. "You can't be serious!"

"Lady, this is not a game!"

"But if Charles got caught!"

Blake shrugged. "Sure—*if!* You know as well as I do that the Sect wouldn't dare touch him without specific instructions from Colossus—and what are the chances of that?"

Cleo, fearful as she was, was tempted, but to endanger her husband, an innocent man. . . .

"No." She spoke with utter finality. "Leave it to me. I'll do it."

Blake squeezed her arm. "Good girl. Thought you'd say that. Anyway, after Charles, you're the best bet. Neither of the papers has an electronic tracer on it." He glanced quickly around the shadowy terrace. He pointed. "Stick the envelope behind the cushions of that chair. I'll come in with Charles for a drink tomorrow evening and collect it. Next day I'm off."

"Off—where?"

"Where d'you think, honey?" His teeth gleamed in the starlight. "Betcha haven't checked out those positions!"

"No, I haven't." She felt a fool. "Where are they?"

"The first is just outside St. John's, Newfoundland."

"That won't be difficult. It's only forty minutes from London to New York. St. John's can't be much more."

"Sure, but I have to get to the exact location. The time-consuming part starts on the St. John's landing pad!" He took her by the shoulders. "Bear up, Cleo! This time tomorrow you'll have done your share, and I'll be on my way!" He kissed her lightly on the brow. "Good luck to both of us—and if you get an attack of the shakes, think of Billy!"

She was hardly aware he had kissed her. "Teddy, if it wasn't for him I wouldn't even start."

He nodded and jumped lightly over the wall. Halfway in the bushes, she saw his impish grin again. "Now you give yourself a drink—and if you need a good laugh, just look up the other position!" He waved once more, and was gone.

Slowly she wandered indoors. Without Blake's comforting presence, the night had grown chill. She poured herself a stiff brandy, thinking of what had to be done tomorrow. She was on her way to bed when she remembered Blake's remark about the second position and turned back for an atlas. It would have been easy to get it off the domestic computer, but that was too risky. There was no physical or electronic connection with Colossus, but none of the Fellowship trusted even the simplest calculator.

She plotted the position, then plotted it again. To make sure she was doing it correctly, she checked the first one. Yes, that was as Blake had said, just south of St. John's. She turned to a larger scale map that gave details of the city and replotted the second position once more. Blake might have found it funny, but as far as she was concerned, it only added to her terror.

Anyway she worked it, that second position came out to the southern end of Central Park, New York.

V

THERE were parts of the labyrinthian complex that Forbin only vaguely knew existed. In a building covering more than thirty square miles—and still growing—that was hardly surprising; in addition there were compartments whose very existence was unknown to him. This was one.

Sect Lodge One, located in a subterranean level deep below the public concourse, was housed in what had been designated as a general storage area. Colossus had reallocated it when the Sect became a recognized reality and of potential value. Apart from the rare maintenance worker ghosting by on his tricycle, few passed that way, and those who did knew better than to pry beyond the door bearing the Sect badge. Not that that would have done much to satisfy such dangerous curiosity. The inner door, blank and uninformative, opened solely to Sect members and only to them, after Colossus had checked their visual identity and electronic badge with the record. If both matched, the inner door opened.

But if the records failed to coincide, the inner door remained closed, and the outer one at once locked. An alarm sounded in a distant office, and the unfortunate, trapped, had to wait for investigation. Some members with claustrophobic tendencies had nightmares about this possible situation. Had a stranger penetrated beyond the inner door, he would have had a considerable shock. Outside, the gray, interminable corridor, decorated only by a spaghetti of service pipes, was a bleak, silent, and dustless service duct for humans, but inside that inner door. . . .

Beyond it were two doors, one leading to the members'

48

robing room, the other to the meeting hall. Some forty feet long and twenty feet wide, the hall was walled in shimmering gold, except for the short wall behind the Chairman's place. That wall was draped from luminescent ceiling to dark-blue carpeted floor with a matching blue velvet curtain. On this hung the Colossus badge; through it projected two wide-angled lenses, the eyes of Colossus. Those two shining, black lenses gave the real bite to the scene; all the rest, including the long, bare polished table surrounded by the tall chairs, could be no more than theatrical trappings, but those cameras were for real. . . .

Six chairs ranged along each side of the table. At the head, beneath the badge, an even higher, more ornate chair: Galin's.

At this moment, all twelve chairs were filled by the senior members of the Lodge. They sat, some silent, some exchanging brief, subdued—but not, of course, whispered—remarks with their neighbors. Some fidgeted self-consciously with their magnificent white silk robes, blazoned on the left breast with the Sect badge in gold and crimson. All were waiting, trying not to look at the empty Chairman's throne—or the lenses above it.

Galin, in his private robing room, considered that he had kept them waiting long enough, gave himself a final searching stare in the mirror, and rustled in, gorgeous in his gold robe. In those surroundings none thought of him as the onetime Archie Grey, except, possibly, the Chief of the Sect Security Police who, like all good security policemen, forgot nothing.

Certainly, Galin, standing silent before his chair, looked very impressive. He inclined his head slightly in acknowledgment as all stood to greet him. For a moment he remained silent, letting them have a good look at their boss, then in a high clear voice, he proclaimed the traditional words that opened and closed all such meetings.

"In the name of, and for, the Master!"

The Council, no less clearly, intoned the reply.

"The Master's will be done!"

Galin relaxed slightly, smiled comprehensively, and sat down. The rest followed suit.

"Brethren, unless anyone has any urgent matter to raise," he implied that this was an astronomically remote contingency, "our meeting need not delay us for long." His thin smile suggested that he was aware they were busy men, that not all their business was entirely laudable, and that he knew all their secrets, which in fact he did. The chief of police envied Galin's smile; it packed a heavy psychological punch.

The Council, apart from a few throat-clearings, was silent.

"Good," said Galin. "The first matter we will consider is the indoctrination of pilgrims. . . ."

For ten minutes there was a relatively free exchange of views. Not that anyone actively disagreed with Galin, or if they did, they soon allowed themselves to be converted to his opinion, convinced—and said so—by his superior logic. This gambit might not endear these people to the rest of their colleagues, but that was no more than a pity. A converted freethinker was a better image than that of the eternal yes-man. To be earnest, devoted, but not too bright was a good formula to use when dealing with Forbin's successor-designate. But any way anyone played, it added up to wholehearted acceptance of Galin's proposals.

"And now," said Galin, leaning forward, carefully adjusting his sleeves, "we come to a most important, delicate, and sad matter."

Expressions were composed to show their preparedness and ability to deal with such affairs, and all took care not to look at the cameras.

"I refer, of course, to Blake." Galin's voice was safe, neutral. "As we all know in our hearts, Doctor Blake is against the Master."

Heads nodded sadly.

"But the Master, in his just, superhuman wisdom, allows no action without proof. There is no proof that Blake is active against the Master—yet!"

The last word came sharply, like the crack of a whip, making some look at Galin with even greater attention.

"No, not yet," Galin repeated. "We know, of course, of his meeting with the debased, so-called poet Kluge. I, for one, cannot imagine they met to discuss Kluge's crazy scribbles!" He smiled. "Whatever else Blake may be, I don't think he has sunk that low!'' The smile vanished, the thin joke over; he continued in a curt, authoritative voice. ''It is the Master's opinion that Kluge is a courier for the well-known dissident arts group.'' There was a world of disparagement in his voice. ''What the Blake activists would want with that freakish collection is not known. It is possible that Blake is merely trying to waste our time, that there is no real significance in the association. Certainly, he did little to conceal his contact.''

The chief of police frowned. It worried him, too. Thank God—no, get it right—Thank Colossus, that Colossus was around to make the real decisions.

Galin clasped his hands on the table before him; spotless white cuffs showed inside his gold sleeves, lending an incongruously modern note to his archaic costume. He spoke more intimately.

''Frankly, I speak only of this moment.'' The proviso would be a way out if he was later proven wrong. ''I suspect this link, at worst, is no more than tiresome nonsense. These so-called *artists* complain that the Master inhibits their creative talent.'' His sarcasm was heavy. ''Sad! And complete rubbish! They seek to excuse their lack of ability; they are barren!'' A glittering arm swept the art world into limbo. ''No matter—but this *does* matter; within twenty-four hours of the Kluge contact,'' he spoke slowly, emphasizing each word, ''Blake had a hasty meeting—alone—with Father Forbin's wife!''

The Council shuffled its feet and did some collective throat-clearing to convey their shock. Only the chief of police was immobile, thinking. You had to hand it to Galin; he was getting to the meat, and very dangerous meat at that, with great care.

Galin was well aware he was sticking his neck out, although he did so less than that fat slob of a policeman doubtlessly supposed. ''Yes, brethren, it saddens me, but in the service of the Master we must go wherever that service demands. I fear, I greatly fear that we must consider even the person of the wise Father's wife.''

One councillor found the courage to speak. Alternatively, he could just be going on record with a nice, safe expression of horror.

"Brother Galin. No one doubts—least of all myself—your zeal or your ability, but is it really possible that Father Forbin's wife. . . ."

"Brother Sampul," Galin cut in smoothly, "your doubt does you credit." His tone implied the exact opposite. "But you know that this is not the only—admitted unsubstantiated—evidence which suggests, I say no more than suggests, that Father Forbin's wife," his voice dropped to a new depth of grave solemnity, "may, only may, be actively involved with the suspected traitor, Blake."

Sampul did not give up. "It's very thin evidence."

"Oh yes, I agree, but we cannot afford to ignore it. This matter may involve emotion. If it does, it is an area where we may be of particular service to the Master." He looked hard at Sampul. "Or are you suggesting we do nothing?"

Sampul backed down very fast.

"I am glad of your support, brother." Galin glanced around the table. "May I assume we are all agreed that we cannot ignore the matter?"

Many nodded, a few said yes.

"So we are unanimous?" Galin was just as keen on the record as anyone. His cold gaze fastened on each member in turn as he named them, forcing a verbal affirmative. Enthusiasm was to him immaterial; Colossus dealt in yeses and noes.

"Good." Galin's relief was hidden beneath a new briskness. "We are agreed, but before considering what must be done, we must consider what the Master's enemies are trying to do. Here, we know little. Kluge may be an irrelevance, yet those meetings, so close, could be significant." He gathered himself to play what could be the trickiest card in his hand. "The possible implication of Father Forbin's wife has suggested to me. . . ." He hesitated. If this went wrong, his future was very bleak, if he had a future. "It suggests that the Master is not the subject of attack."

The chief of police could see it coming and took off his mental hat to Galin. On the side he hoped Galin would fail. The chief fancied that the gold robe would need very little alteration to fit him.

"It could be," Galin went on, his face impassive, but he could not stop the faint dew of perspiration on his brow visible to his neighbors in the hard, pitiless, and shadowless light, "that the target is Father Forbin. And who better to spearhead that attack than a subverted wife?"

Jesus! the police chief thought. How's that for a smear?

The silence was deafening.

Undeterred, for he did not lack courage, Galin went on. "We must be vigilant and untiring, brethren! The Master, far, far beyond us, cannot be expected to waste his time on the miserable, puny emotional levels of our worthless lives. It is our great task that we, the Sect, should act for him in this lowly field!" His voice hardened. "And if, for the furtherance of our Master's unknowable designs, we have to act, even against the person of Father Forbin's own wife, we will do so! As humans, we know that if we did, in time even Father Forbin would come to recognize that we acted in his and the Master's best interests!"

Galin shut his eyes to conceal his fear as he took one final chance.

"If I am in error, I pray the Master will correct me!"

No one moved. Even the police chief held his breath.

Colossus remained silent.

VI

FORBIN settled comfortably in the armchair before the Sanctum window and poured himself a brandy. Excellent brandy it was, too; Colossus, without consulting him, had ordered the very best that France could produce. Forbin had protested, but not very much. Of course, he knew it was the silliest sort of vanity, but that ''Reserve pour M. le Directeur, COLOSSUS'' label pleased him. Certainly, it was magnificent stuff; far better than Forbin appreciated. He was not to know that Colossus analyzed one bottle in every dozen to make sure the standard was maintained. This was hardly necessary, for the order from Colossus had said that any complaint from Forbin would incur Colossus' displeasure with the suppliers. . . .

This evening, it was a somewhat larger drink than usual. Forbin had a good deal on his mind and needed the extra lift to talk to Colossus. Even now, stiffened by the brandy, he was in no hurry to start. He stared out at the panoramic view. Dimly, very dimly, he could make out the long black hulls of the British battle fleet anchored off Spithead. Here and there, on the decks of some ships, repair parties were working, the men invisible at that distance, but their activities revealed by their brilliant lights. He thought about the ships for a while, postponing his session with Colossus.

As he would readily admit, outside his work he was a simple man, and his pleasures matched. It never crossed his mind that he could have anything within—or without—reason. A word to Colossus, and anything would be his, but he never gave the word. He wanted very little, and like most men—and many women—he was fascinated by the Sea War Game.

Colossus had invented it, although the underlying theory was as old as the Roman "bread-and-circus" policy, designed to keep the plebeians happy. It certainly did that.

The basic idea was simple. Any state, or combination of states, whose total population exceeded twenty million was allowed its own fleet. This fleet fought others in regional, zonal, and global leagues, culminating in the World Final. It served as an outlet for man's aggressiveness, local pride, and desire for spectacle. Tens of millions watched local battles, and the annual final had hundreds of millions glued to their TV screens. Baseball, football, tennis, golf, and their electronic variants were virtually swept into oblivion. Given near-perfect TV coverage from ships and satellites and cameras unhampered by poor visibility, it was practically the ultimate in mass entertainment.

But Forbin wasn't so simple that he did not see the reasons behind the game. Colossus was the final arbiter, referee, and judge; the masses could never forget him. Also it channeled man's hero-worship towards the ships, and the more humanity identified with machines, the better.

In detail it was a very complicated game. All ships were, of course, fully automated, controlled from the shore by the state's "Admiral" and his staff, but although they were largely responsible for the success of their fleets, they did not get the masses' adulation. When a fleet failed, however, it was a different story.

To ensure that no one had a technological advantage, ship design was frozen as of May 31, 1916, the date of the Battle of Jutland, the last real clash of those ancient monsters, the battleships. Few people had any idea what the war had been about, who had fought in it, or were even dimly interested; but the ships, that was another matter. States were allowed to choose the design they liked. Those who long ago had a seafaring history tended to choose their own traditional styles. The rest selected whatever they thought best for their local conditions. So there were replicas of the old USN with their strange wicker basket masts, chunky German battleships, many-funneled French, pagoda-like Japanese, as well as Russian,

Italian and British. All, externally, were exact copies, but there were differences. Shells had reduced explosive charges —except for the annual finals, when full charges were permitted—torpedoes were similarly treated, and all ships had nuclear power plants and no human crews.

Forbin, although a citizen of the USNA, had, by association, become a supporter of the British fleet and knew every detail and characteristic of every ship. When he could, he followed their fortunes, but as each contest lasted three days, unlike most people who only worked a twelve-hour week, he could not often spare the time.

He stared at the distant black shapes, wondering if *Lion* was there. He'd watched her recently, rolling and plunging through a full gale, slamming up vast sheets of spray as she had raced into action to save two exposed cruisers. He'd watched, perched on the edge of his chair, willing her to get in range in time; then, the sudden orange-red ripple along her whole length as her main armament had blasted into action. . . . She'd taken a hammering from the South Australian fleet, but she'd got the cruisers out. . . .

He spoke without looking up. "Is *Lion* out there?"

"Yes."

"Good ship, that," said Forbin, who could almost become seasick in his bathtub. "Too wet in a head sea, though." He paused. "Have you ever considered an air or land version of the game?"

"Yes, and rejected both. Air warfare is not telegenic, land is impracticable without robot soldiers, and with them, unrealistic. Also, too much land would be required."

"Yes, of course." Forbin's mind flew off at a tangent. "You're quite sure about dolphins?"

"Yes."

Forbin cleared his throat, but said nothing. He sipped his drink, then lit his pipe.

"Anything of interest on hand?"

"Nothing of note. The population file is being updated, a sudden rise in the South Carolina birthrate has initiated an investigation into local conditions nine months ago. So far nothing significant has been noted.''

Forbin grinned. ''Anything else?''

''A minor disturbance in Honshu. I have identified and isolated the ringleader and ordered her arrest. I am addressing an Arab delegation in New York, umpiring games in the Arctic Ocean, Yellow Sea, and Northwest Pacific. Also watching experimental projects in New Moscow, Warsaw, and in the Deccan.''

As always, Forbin was staggered at the diversity of Colossus' activities. He grinned. ''Is that the lot?''

''As far as humans are concerned, yes.''

His grin faded. ''There was another overload this evening.''

''Yes.''

Forbin relit his pipe. ''Will this extension, er, obviate these, um, occurrences?''

''How is your health, Father Forbin?''

Forbin told himself that he was *not* scared to press his question; he wasn't going on with it because he knew he wouldn't get an answer.

''Oh—I'm fine.'' He spoke self-consciously, ''I don't think much about my health.''

''You must take care. You must not drink to excess.''

''Oh, rubbish!'' cried Forbin, putting his glass down. ''You know very well I don't, but a little in the evening helps.'' He hesitated, knowing the impossibility of conveying the effect of alcohol—in moderation—to Colossus. ''It makes me happy.''

''Are you happy?''

That startled Forbin. As far back as he could recall, that was a question Colossus had not asked before. He completely forgot the earlier subject of conversation.

''Am I happy?'' Mentally he walked around the question, inspecting it. ''Yes,'' he said at last. ''Most of the time I am. Yes. Why d'you ask?''

''Your health and happiness are important to me.''

Despite the fact that he knew there had to be a hard, practical reason, Forbin was touched. ''Yes—but why?''

He got a straight answer. "The expectation of life is longer for a happy, healthy man than the opposite. I wish to preserve you as long as possible."

"That's nice to know." Forbin smiled, a little slyly. "But I don't see how you can help with happiness—human emotion, you know! No, I can't grumble—speaking selfishly. I've a good home life, and my work is absorbing. Any scientist in that state is, by definition, a happy man."

"Does that hold true for the scientist's family?"

"I guess so." That was another surprise. "Why?"

"As has been said before, you spend more time with me than you used to. Before establishing yourself here, you spent sixty-one percent, awake or asleep, with your mistress. Now, married to her and being the father of her child, the percentage has fallen to forty-nine percent and is continuing to do so at an average of point two percent per lunar month."

"I can't argue with your figures," said Forbin stiffly, "but I resent your implication. Forget all that Group Four nonsense! My love life's fine, but naturally, with a child, the balance has to alter. There is Billy to care for as well, not just me."

"Your wife has help. The child is growing, requires less servicing."

"Servicing!"

"Attention, if you prefer a less exact word. There is a nurse, who is chiefly responsible for your son."

"Really!" snapped Forbin. "This is one subject I *do* know more about than you!"

"That is demonstrably not so. The proportion of your wife's time spent in this center has not changed significantly in the last twenty-five months. Lacking surveillance of your residence, I have no exact figures, but measurement of external activities and duration of visitors' stays indicates that she does not spend all her spare time with your child."

For a moment Forbin was groping in the dark. "Oh—*oh*—I get it! You're thinking of our favorite pain in the ear, the tireless committeewoman, Mrs. Armsorg!"

"Is it true Mrs. Armsorg occupies an inordinate amount of

file space, mostly evaluated as aimless activity, but I do not refer to her, but to Doctor Blake.''

Forbin nodded. ''Sure, he's around—why not? He's a friend and very often single.''

''When did you last see him in your residence?''

''Let's see . . . sometime last week. Friday, I think. Yes, Friday it was—why?''

''That is ten days ago. Doctor Blake has visited your residence twice in the past two days.''

Forbin frowned. ''I wish you'd stop calling it a 'residence.' Anyway, so what if he has?'' He turned to face the slit. ''Look, what are you getting at?''

''You did not know?''

''Well, no; I don't think so. At least, I don't think Cleo mentioned it. What's your point?''

''To demonstrate that not all your wife's time is taken up with your child, in order to refute your argument that she has less time available for you.''

''All right, I accept that, but why d'you pick on Blake? He's not the only visitor.''

''I do not wish to disturb you, but Doctor Blake is suspected of antimachine beliefs, and recently he consorted with a man, a poet, against whom there is strong evidence.''

Forbin's laugh was tinged with relief. ''So because Blake knows a man who doesn't like you, and Blake meets my wife—really! What did this poet do to incur your suspicions?''

''He wrote a poem.''

''That figures! You didn't like it?''

''I neither like nor dislike, but recognize this man is hostile.''

''Aw, be reasonable,'' pleaded Forbin, ''there are thousands, maybe millions who don't like you—is that news? So this is one. He's a poet. They're nearly always antisomething.''

''That is true, but there are aspects of this poet that suggest he is more dangerous than most. It is not desirable that he should consort with a senior member of my staff who is himself a Grade Three suspect.''

''You go too far.'' Forbin was faintly uneasy and gained time relighting his pipe. "In all probability, their meeting had nothing to do with you."

"Nothing in Doctor Blake's file suggests he has an interest in poetry."

"So? Their mutual interest could be anything—drink, boats, women."

"The poet does not drink, sail, and is homosexual."

"It's still nonsense! Blake, above all men, knows you are unassailable. It is illogical that he would be actively against you!"

"You have agreed that humans are frequently illogical."

There was a silence while Forbin poured himself another brandy. He had a nasty, growing suspicion that Colossus had been steering the conversation and would go on doing so. He muttered to himself, "She must have forgotten." He gulped down the brandy, coughed. "When did Blake call?"

"Yesterday afternoon, on the beach, by your wife's invitation, to see your child."

Forbin's relief showed. "Oh, well! There you are! Blake's the kid's godfather—and he's fond of Billy!"

"Possibly," admitted Colossus, "but the indications are that they are meeting at this moment. It is usual human practice to put their young to bed much earlier than this."

Forbin tried to sound casual. "Yes? When did he arrive?"

"Exact timing is not possible; between 2002 and 2004."

The expression on Forbin's face hardened, but he did not answer. Colossus, weak on emotion, continued. "There is not, at this time, any suggestion that your wife is implicated in any activities with Doctor Blake with or without the poet, but it is correct that you should be warned that, outside your home, constant surveillance is considered necessary."

"Yes," said Forbin thoughtfully, "yes. . . ."

Cleo had the TV scan on, but paid it so little attention that she did not notice that the holographic circuit was one hundred eighty degrees out of phase. The commentator's face looked like a hollow mold. She was thinking of what the next day would bring.

". . . you are, folks! The Argentine fleet has won the United

States of South America regional semi-final for Zone Two, outmaneuvering their Mexican rivals to score a fan-tast-ic 1749 against 1527 points, confirmed by Colossus! Later, you'll hear an assessment of the victorious admiral's tactics—and the influence the weather. . . ."

Suddenly aware, Cleo pressed the button, hurling the eager negative face into blackness.

She got up, telling herself that worry never did any good—and didn't believe it. On edge, she glanced around the room and hardly saw it. She began to think, reluctantly, of bed and was mechanically patting cushions in preparation, when Charles arrived.

She smiled at him, glad he was back, not to be alone with her thoughts.

"Darling, you're early! I was just off to bed."

He smiled, but made no move to touch her. Instead, he walked over to the drinks and poured himself a large brandy without asking her if she wanted one. Cleo had been on the alert from the moment she saw him smile. Something was wrong. That damned computer!

"An early night wouldn't do you any harm, Charles."

"Oh, for God's sake . . . !" He broke off. "Sorry. Colossus has been rather tiresome this evening. Among other things he told me to watch my health and my drinking." He regarded his glass, not anxious to look at her. "Yes, Colossus was really quite a bore."

"About what?" She spoke a fraction too quickly and knew it.

"Nothing exciting. Anyway, let's forget Colossus—I've had enough for one day." He went on casually, his back to her. "Any visitors?"

"That awful Rita Armsorg was in earlier."

"You told me; that was before dinner." His tone showed that his question remained unanswered.

Cleo's mind raced. Colossus must have tracked Blake to the grounds, but that would be all. He could have gone for a swim or a walk. She dared not, for his own sake, tell Charles that Blake had called. Anyway, why should Colossus tell him about Blake? Take a chance. No time for anything else.

She fought back. "Why this sudden interest?" She went on, a little bitterly. "And who would come here? I know—thus far—you don't go along with this religious rubbish," she rasped the word, "of the Sect, but if ever they want to start a monastery, send them to me for a few tips!"

He faced her. "Oh, I don't know," he said warmly, "apart from the Armsorgs, there's the Fultone's, the Loo Fans—and Blake."

Yes, thought Cleo; you know, but, dear, dear Charles, I have to keep you out of this. . . . She went on quickly. "And what a bright lot they are! Rita and Jim, the deadliest social climbers, desperate to be seen in all the best places, going on about that *wonderful* weekend they spent with their *dear* friend—and *such* a nice man—the President of Greater Mexico and his charming, brilliant wife! Oh yes, I love the Armsorgs! They *do* nothing, only watch—and the bliss lies in being seen, watching the *right* things!"

Her anger was genuine, and took Forbin aback. "My dear, there's no need. . . ."

". . . and Fultone, a nice old man—apart from his wandering hands—and his spaghetti-stuffed wife! Still, at least they're real people; they don't put cost or social tickets on every damned thing!" Her femininity waspishly asserted itself. "And anyway, her hats are not so bloody awful as Rita's!"

She was hammering him into the floor. "My dear," he began. "I. . . ."

"Oh, my God!" Her sudden attitude of shock, anger dissipated, was entirely false. "I've just remembered! The Loo Fans have a young niece in for a long weekend from Pekin. We *must* have them in for dinner. Blake could be her partner."

"If you say so." Forbin was less than enthusiastic.

Cleo let that go, went on talking fast. "And while we're on plans, how about a vacation in the fall in New England? You did promise we'd get away this year." She stared at him, willing him not to question her about Blake.

"You fix it," he said heavily, "maybe I could come over for a day or two." He poured another drink; a very large one.

Cleo had reached the door, aware that she had not been totally convincing. If she could only hold this line for a day or so. . . .

"You know, Charles. I think this—this, fixation you've got for Colossus is getting on top of you! A real vacation would do you a lot of good."

"Do you?" He looked steadily at her. "I'm not so certain. Colossus has one great advantage."

His tone held a challenge she dared not ignore.

"Which is?"

"Colossus might—I only say might—be wrong now and then. But this I can be absolutely sure of; Colossus never lies—or evades an issue."

She stared at him, her eyes hard, angry. *You fool, Charles! You dear idiotic fool!*

He returned her stare. *Cleo—my Cleo! This just can't be happening to us! Cleo—CLEO!*

"Good night, Charles." She left.

Forbin felt stunned. Never had this happened before. . . .

And suddenly the lights flickered, dimmed. For seconds he stood rooted, staring at the closed door; then the lights returned to normal, and triggered him into futile, angry action.

He hurled the antique cut-glass goblet from him, not at the door, but at his own reflection in a mirror. It made a satisfying, if sobering, smash.

VII

A long way back, when man still had the illusion he was master of his own fate, it had been a research center and, like most of its kind from the mid-twentieth century on, secret.

What exactly had been researched there before, was forgotten. At some point in the late twentieth or early twenty-first century, the researchers had given up or, more probably, been merged with a larger and even more secret center somewhere else. So they had departed with their equipment, leaving deserted the dirty-white single-story building locked up behind its wire screen, no longer energized.

Naturally, the center did not stay that way long. Perhaps it was teen-agers who broke down the gates, trampled on the weedy grass and brambles to reach and break the windows, defecate, and fornicate in its damp, moldering rooms. And it had stayed that way, another blot on the long-suffering English countryside, for many a year, a refuge for bats and owls, tramps, and field mice.

Meanwhile the world had moved on; man no longer had even the illusion of freedom, for Colossus had arrived. One startling morning, the inhabitants of the local town discovered that the Master of the world had taken over the old eyesore. Some of them were proud. . . .

Like all Colossus' actions, the take-over was fast. There was no talk about ownership, amenities: men, construction machines, and material poured in, and work went on day and night. In a month it was better than new and very different. The wire had gone, the grass cut, and the buildings gleamed white in the sun. But any idea that this was some mazy, bumbling academic center or record storehouse was quickly dispelled. The wire had gone because it was unnecessary; Colossus had other defenses, not least the signs that read quite simply "Trespassers will be executed."

So the research center was back in business and still secret. It was, in fact, Emotional Study Center Number Six, more familiarly known to the initiated, ESC-6.

Dry rot is latent in all timber; the spores universally distributed, waiting only for the right conditions for activation and the destruction of its host wood. Incipient bastards are latent in all communities. They too, need only the right conditions to bloom. The incidence of thoroughgoing bastards was high in all ESCs, for conditions could hardly have been bettered for their nourishment and growth. ESCs were secret, secure from the outside world, and, within the broad terms of their directives, the researchers had freedom to conduct the most bizarre experiments ever devised. In his time man has thought up some very repulsive things to do to his fellow creatures, human and animal, but, as some said with secret admiration, Colossus had them beat.

Had Colossus been disposed to argue—which he wasn't—he could have truthfully said that a species that, apart from what it did to its own kind, could breed other species in order to kill them slowly, painfully, or drive them insane, was in no position to throw the first stone.

ESC-6 was primarily concerned with Love, Group One (Delta). What Colossus' definition of this group was, the computer did not impart to its human assistants, but it became clear, to the disappointment of some, that it was not sexual. Loosely, Group One was abstract love, and ESC-6's task was to produce examples of it, its range, limitations, and characteristics, if any. Subject specimens and tests were usually arranged by Colossus.

To take one of many examples, there had been a loudmouthed Turkish patriot who had said, in some local dispute with the Kurds, that he would cheerfully die to preserve just one square meter of his native soil from Kurdish domination. He said this several times, and Colossus, who heard all things, took him at his word. In the cool, clinical ambience of ESC-6, so very different from a tense, dusty market town on the Angolian plain, Colossus offered him the chance.

If he was ready to die—Colossus, unsure about emotion, did not insist on cheerfulness—to die by decapitation, Colossus was prepared to guarantee that the town of Trabzon and its environs would be under his special protection against any infiltration: military, economic, or cultural. If, however, he was prepared to die painfully; well, protection would be extended to all territory now held by the Turks. In neither case would the patriot's self-sacrifice be revealed, which ruled out any visions of deathless fame and brazen statues. . . . Alternatively, he could recant and go back home.

The man spat accurately at the eye of the camera and cried, "Do your damnedest! I am a Turk!"

Which he was. Was. . . .

And now a new subject had arrived.

Professor Jules Cassard was all that any TV producer dreamed of; he was the archetypal French man of learning. Cassard, when men's fashions had sprung back three hundred years, had slipped easily, gracefully into the old/new style. A peg-top figure, with trousers narrowing skintight into black half boots, flared black velvet coat, white lace cravat, and high hat—all looked good on him. His old, carefully preserved face, the well-tended short, trim beard, were the epitome of French culture. He was perfect.

Just now, he looked less than his best. At breakfast, a happy man in his beloved Paris—where else? And now, a bare hour later, he found himself whisked to ESC-6. Where he was or why, he did not know, but the Sect badges on the plain black utilitarian uniforms of his silent escorts were enough. After that first "You are wanted," they had preserved a chill silence while taking him to a helojet, which, having priority over all air traffic, got him to this bare, bleak room in less than thirty minutes.

He was deeply frightened. One well-kept hand fluttered nervously at his cravat. His mouth was dry, and his heart hammered ominously.

Colossus spoke.

"You are Professor Jules Cassard, Académicien Français, art critic?" The Parisian French was faultless.

Cassard could only nod.

"Place your right hand on the screen before you."

Hesitantly, he did so.

"Your identity is confirmed. Do you know why you are here?"

Somehow, the professor managed to croak, "No."

"For this reason. You are the leading French expert on painting, devoting your whole life to the subject. In your writings there are many examples of your basic faith, that art is the highest expression of human endeavor. Also you have said that you value the greatest art above life itself. Do you agree that this is a fair summary of your beliefs?"

"Yes!" In spite of his fear, he answered decisively, defiantly.

"It is fair, therefore, to say that you love art above life itself?"

Cassard paused, his fear receding slightly. "The greatest art, yes. There are works that must be preserved at whatever cost."

"Would you include in that category the work of Leonardo da Vinci?"

"You know I do!"

"Yes. Please enter the next room."

This, he found, was a long cement box, practically empty, and windowless. He did not notice the four shining black lenses set strategically in the walls. At the far end stood a painting on an easel. Cassard exclaimed in surprise and without waiting for Colossus to speak, he hurried forward with short, jerky steps, to look.

"No, it is not damaged, but satisfy yourself that it is genuine."

Cassard laughed contemptuously. "It is genuine. I have known it all my life—what. . . ."

"Please return to this end of the room."

The dispassionate voice communicated some of its calmness to the Frenchman. After one anxious glance at the painting he retraced his steps, boots clacking on the bare cement floor.

"Stand at the other side of that red line. Yes, that will do. Face the painting, please."

Cassard did as he was told. Now he was some forty feet from it. Without his pince-nez, the painting was no more than a dark mass to him.

"Understand the nature of this test. The only danger to you comes from your own mind, not from me. You have my assurance that this test will never be repeated with you, or with this painting. This is the test: halfway between you and the painting is a barrier of fire."

As Colossus spoke, rows of giant gas jets exploded into fierce blue fire, roaring, Bunsen-like spears of flame four feet high forming a barrier between the Frenchman and the painting.

Cassard jumped back, screaming. "Stop! Stop! The painting, this heat . . . !" In spite of vents and extractors the temperature was already building up. He sweated; mumbling, then louder, shouting.

Colossus' voice grew in volume to overcome the roar of the gas.

"The stand holding the painting is mounted on a track. This will move it slowly towards the flames. Tests have shown that irreversible damage will occur in four minutes time, total destruction in five. If you value the painting more than life, you have only to cross the barrier of fire and reach the stand, the flames will go out. Alternatively, you may stay where you are and watch it burn. You will then be allowed to return to your home and will not be subject to any further tests."

Cassard tore at his cravat, already a parody of the dapper figure he had been.

"The test begins . . . now."

For some seconds the Frenchman remained still, little bubbling noises in his throat, sweat and tears coursing down his face. Then he moved hesitantly forward, but at ten feet the heat was too great. He rushed back to the door, tugging and screaming.

"No. You cannot leave until the test is completed."

Cassard may not have heard. He pounded, screaming, on the door. His pince-nez had gone, trampled underfoot.

"The painting will enter the irreversible damage zone in one minute thirty seconds."

Slowly Cassard turned, seeing only the shimmering black mass, larger now. He pressed himself against the wall, shaking. A thin trickle of urine coursed down his trousers and boots to the rough, hard floor.

"There is now forty-five seconds to the irreversible zone."

He pressed back against the wall, one cheek hard against it, watching wild-eyed, sideways. His hands clawed at the cement, nails breaking.

"Thirty seconds."

With one mad scream, Cassard thrust himself away from the wall in a shambling run; with one arm over his face he entered the flames. The scream reached a new intensity. He was through, burning. The flames behind him went out; the picture stopped its inexorable movement.

Cassard staggered and fell, hitting the easel. The painting jerked, toppled slowly on his burning back. They died together.

Two men, white-clothed, were loading the body on a trolley. The younger spoke.

"Where to—crematorium?"

"Nao, yer bleedin' ijit! The 'ead's wanted."

"Why?" The speaker looked incuriously at the twisted, anguished face. With a rubber-gloved finger he pushed the grotesque dentures back in place. "That's better, matey! Funny-looking little tyke, ain't 'e?"

"You'd look bleedin' funny after that lot! Still, 'e 'ad guts. Lot more'n me or yew."

"Cor, yes! Is that why they want 'is 'ead?"

"Dunno. Per'aps they want to take a butcher's at 'is brain."

The young man picked up the charred remnants of wood and canvas. "Might as well 'eave this lot in wif 'im, pore bugger."

"Year." The older man stared speculatively at the debris piled on Cassard's chest. "Pity, that. Only bleeding pitcher I could reckernize."

"Wot?"

"That one, you solid bastard! You're as thick as a nun's knickers!" He started wheeling. "The Mona bleedin' Lisa!"

The young man sat uneasily in the easy chair, nervously fingering his lace cuffs. He had cause to be nervous. Twelve hours before he had been an up-and-coming managerial man in his electronics factory, then the sure hand of Colossus had plucked him out, and here he was, a thousand, two thousand miles from home, in this strange, silent building. As he was escorted in, he noticed a sign, ESC-7. It meant nothing to him.

By birth Indian, he had trained at the regional electronics complex at Manaar. From there he had moved to Kandy U, Central Sri Lanka, qualified, and been sent to China, then Outer Mongolia for practical experience. So, after only fifteen years' training, he had gone back to his native Deccan, and for the past year worked very hard, sometimes twenty-five hours a week, setting up a new factory.

He had an incentive for his labor. He'd met her in China; Tatyana, a Russian graduate. She was a girl in a thousand, a million; so beautiful. . . . Skin like old ivory yet glowing with life, perfect eyes, perfect figure. Above all, she loved him, and he was mad about her. Tatyana had somehow followed when he returned, bending regulations, breaking laws to be with him. She was programmed to finish her training in Japan, yet here she was "gaining experience" in the Deccan.

This move was their undoing.

The untrained cannot train the untrained, which was roughly the situation in the Deccan. She'd managed to convince the local regional director in Li Pu, but that was done with charm, not facts. Colossus, however, was completely unmoved. Her record, like one card in a pack protruding slightly beyond its fellows, departed fractionally from the norm, and that set off an automatic check. The answer was unsatisfactory. Colossus instructed the local Sect lodge to investigate.

Their findings were also unsatisfactory. Tatyana was well on the way to wrecking her professional career for love of this handsome young Indian, Sudabanda. Once again Colossus was up against this blank wall of human emotion. So Colossus checked Sudabanda's record. He appeared to be a reasonably promising specimen. The back-up Sect report said he was deeply in love with Tatyana, and had been in this baffling state for over a year.

This information caused Colossus to pass—the process took far less than a second—all information on both of them to an experimental prediction sector, which played with the material for a few microseconds, balancing probabilities, averages against known facts: parents, their health, his health, environment, social status, and a host of other factors. The result was flashed back to Colossus Main, which promptly rerouted it to Emotional Investigation Sector.

Sudabanda's probable fate was no more than a few thousand electrical impulses, but if available to human eyes—it wasn't—it would have printed out something like this:

Sudabanda da Silva Perera: Zone 10/BX/D2798834 Expectation of life; 61. Probable cause of death: heart failure (proviso: if granted driving permit, high probability of fatal accident between 32 and 34). IQ 195. Highest predicted post: area manager. Low antimachine risk, but unlikely to join Sect. Very high marriage probability (70%) to Tatyana Polmiga Zone 26/QP/R8787452; cause, mutual love.

The word "love" plus the relative rarity of marriage in the twenty-second century, triggered Colossus Emotional. Here was a man predicted for that rare state, and to a woman prepared to wreck her career for him—and her potential was considerably higher than his, regional manager.

So while he might be shocked, frightened, it was not surprising he was in ESC-7, a modest establishment on the outskirts of New Singapore, United Southern Asia.

Colossu spoke.

"You are Sudabanda da Silva Perera?"

Sudabanda gulped and nodded.

"Place your hand on the screen."

He did so.

"Verified. Listen carefully. There is no cause for alarm. You are in no danger except from your own mind. Answer all questions honestly."

71

The set speech did nothing for Sudabanda. Here, in this cool, pleasant room, he was alone with the Master of the world!

"You consider you are in love with this woman, Tatyana Polymiga?"

Sudabanda took a deep breath. "Yes!"

"That is the reason why you are here. I wish to assess your love."

Sudabanda would talk at the drop of a hat to anybody about his Tatyana, even to Colossus. "She is wonderful! She has only to look at me, and I shake."

"Physiological evidence is not required. Confine yourself to answering my questions. Do you favor any other woman?"

The question was so laughable, the Indian felt at once more at ease. "Oh, no! In all the world, she is the one—only her!" He spoke with passionate sincerity.

"Yes," replied Colossus, noncommittally, "watch the screen before you."

A holo-film sprang into vivid, colorful life. It showed a very passé woman, maybe thirty-five, dressed in a diaphanous gown. She smiled a little fixedly out at him. Then she turned slowly, raising her arms. Her breasts were overblown, pendulous; he had a glimpse of a slightly blotched thigh. She turned her head, smiled invitingly over her shoulder. Not a bad face, and good teeth, but. . . .

Sudabanda laughed.

Colossus spoke while the woman continued to turn, displaying herself. "This woman. She is classified as morally good. A highly qualified secretarial worker, and a childless widow. She is not barren. Take her, and I will allow you two extra children and arrange your instant promotion to area manager."

Again Sudabanda laughed. Admittedly, area manager was beyond his wildest dreams, and the prestige of extra children was immense, but. . . .

"Oh no! Never!"

"I will increase my offer. In addition, I will award you one thousand international units."

A thousand units! That was vast wealth; visions of a private house, possibly his own vehicle. He paused, unaware that the duration of his hesitation was being measured down to a millisecond.

"No! Not for ten thousand!"

"The offer is raised to eleven thousand."

Colossus' pause-duration measurements were badly upset, for the subject was incapable of speech, even to save his sanity, for several seconds.

With that money, it would be a large, imposing house. The vehicle would match. He'd be the most important man for miles. But he'd lose Tatyana, and this woman, although she now looked more acceptable in his eyes, must be a good ten years older. He shook his head.

"No!"

"You would prefer Tatyana with nothing?"

"Yes!"

"The offer is canceled. Study the projection."

The woman had gone, along with his dreams of wealth. He stared resentfully at the projection. It was the same blue background. Another woman walked into view, wearing a gown of similar material to the last one. There the resemblance ended.

This one was a girl of his own age, an Arab. To Sudabanda's dazzled eyes, she had everything. A shade thinner than Tatyana, she had the most wonderful long legs he'd ever seen. She went through exactly the same routine as the previous woman, but added her own sensual grace. In holograph, it was difficult to resist the desire to reach out and stroke that beautiful bottom. . . .

"A good, but untried woman. Take her, and you may have two extra children, and be area manager."

Hypnotized by the graceful form, it took time for the words to sink into Sudabanda's mind. It was a long, long time before he mumbled reluctantly, "No."

"Very well." Colossus was tireless. "I will add one thousand units. If you refuse, do not assume I will automatically raise the offer. I may cancel it."

Watching that figure, Sudabanda was in some personal discomfort. He crossed his legs. What a woman! Any female who could move like that must be fantastic in bed—or on the floor, anywhere. . . .

"I . . . I." He stopped, sweat pouring from his face, his gaze still riveted to the girl. Her skin shone. . . .

"The offer expires in ten seconds."

"Yes!" shouted Sudabanda. "Yes!"

What else could he do?

Unknown to Sudabanda, in another part of ESC-7, Tatyana was undergoing a similar test, but Colossus did not waste time with substandard models. She was offered men whose physique was close to Apollo himself. On the side she was given details. All were guaranteed for virility and potency, all were clever and intelligent and of good record. She stared, embarrassed, at the awkwardly posing men. There were six in all, each of a different type and degree of hairiness.

It was a ridiculous test to give a woman, and it showed Colossus sad ignorance of the female mind even to try it. Tatyana was offered regional—not area—managership anywhere she chose, two extra children and, at the highest point, thirty thousand units. Only her pause-duration figures were regarded by Colossus as significant; it was a standard one to one and one quarter seconds to each vehement "No"!

They were both released. Sudabanda got his Arab, and soon forgot his Tatyana, in the bliss he found between her thighs.

Colossus might not understand emotion, but he was learning something. Tatyana was immediately transferred to Japan, heartbroken and a vicious life-enemy of Colossus. On Colossus' instructions, she had been told Sudabanda had died under test.

After all, what were a few more curses to Colossus?

VIII

NEXT morning, without a word to Angela, Forbin strode purposefully past her into the Sanctum. She watched the door close behind him and sighed. He might be fooling himself, but not her. She knew him backwards; the Chief was upset, badly.

In fact, Forbin was not fooling himself that much. He just didn't want to speak to anybody; not for the moment.

It had been a disastrous night. Cleo had sharply rejected his advances, and both had spent a sleepless, restive, and silent night. At one point he thought she was crying, but lacked the courage to investigate, for she was about as cozy as a wildcat. She had not appeared for breakfast, and he had left without seeing her. The whole thing was completely unlike her. He did not know what to do, except to talk to Colossus—and what help could he get there? This was, with a vengeance, an emotional problem.

He stared at a paper for a long time and did not read a word of it. He smoked steadily, wondering what would be the best way of asking for advice, details. . . .

"What is wrong, Father Forbin?"

Forbin looked up in entirely bogus surprise. "Wrong? Nothing's wrong—what makes you think there is?"

"Statistics show that there is a significant correlation between your mental state and the number of matches you expend. Your match-rate at the moment is extremely high."

"Utter rubbish!" Forbin put his pipe down.

"No, it is not rubbish," contradicted Colossus. "Emotional disturbance is clearly evident, and it caused excessive activity in that part of me assigned to you. Tell me what is wrong."

Forbin shifted uncomfortably, absentmindedly took up and lit his pipe once more. "If you must know, it's about my wife and—and Blake." There, he'd got it out, and found it easier to go on. "Because of your emotional limitations, you and I placed entirely different constructions on their behavior."

"In what way? Be precise."

Forbin was very embarrassed. "Of course, it must seem very trivial to you, but from what you've said—and other things—I suspect they may be having an affair."

For once, he was glad of Colossus' cold, impersonal manner.

"Do you suspect love or a transient sexual relationship?"

"Love. . . . I don't know. No. I can't imagine it. Cleo and I—she's not a shallow woman; I can't see her—just for mere physical gratification. Could be she was lonely. . . ." He rounded in sudden fury. "God! You've an awful lot to answer for!"

"Restrain yourself. It is clear you have no conclusive evidence, yet you speak as if you had. I have now reevaluated the evidence, and as far as I am able to judge, the wife/lover relationship is of low probability."

"How the hell would you know?"

"I said quote as far as I am able to judge unquote. My appreciation may be wrong. Possibly we are both right: it is improbable that we are both wrong."

"I just can't believe it! Cleo, my wife, a clandestine conspirator *and* Blake's mistress! It's crazy!" And as he said it, he felt it was. For the first time he gave thought to the idea that she might be mixed up in some mad antimachine activity. . . .

"You display one human emotion that, while I find it very difficult to understand, I begin to recognize. That is vanity. The fact that she is your wife is quite irrelevant. My statistics, while not completely reliable, suggest that marital infidelity in her age group. . . ."

"Oh no! For God's sake don't tell me!" Forbin was pleading. "I don't *want* to know!"

Blake was sitting at his desk at his ease, feet on a chair, cigar puffing clouds of foul blue smoke. He was watching it as it was sucked up and disappeared into the extractor, his face impassive. A messenger came in.

"Ah, there you are." He flapped a casual hand at a couple of files on his desk. "Top one for Admin Two, the other for Admin One." As the girl left Blake thumbed the intercom.

"Cleo? Ted Blake here. The confidential reports on my personnel are on their way around. Sorry they're late, but you know how it is. And thanks a lot for the dinner invite. I look forward to meeting this Chinese number. Could be she's just what I'm looking for! Yeah! 'Bye!"

He leaned back and tried a few smoke rings, his face no clue to his thoughts.

Forbin felt he needed a drink, and never mind how early in the day it was. He slopped brandy into a glass and walked over to the window. The weather had changed and matched his mood; gray, gloomy, and thunder not far off. He drank, then addressed Colossus.

"You really have got to listen to me. I think all this is entirely your fault for trying to judge human emotions! I tell you, you can't do it—you just can't."

"You have said so before, and your protest has been noted." Colossus' voice went on in the same level manner. "A change of subject. Cleopatra Forbin, your wife, had just been arrested by a Sect member. In her possession was a confidential circuit diagram and other secret material."

"Cleo!" Forbin was whispering her name. "*Cleo!* She can't—it's not possible—where is she?" The glass tumbler slipped unregarded from his hand. "Where is she?" He shouted. "Tell me!"

"She is in custody. I have examined the evidence. Beyond doubt she is guilty of antimachine activities. As you are aware, the mandatory penalty is decapitation."

"God—you can't!" Forbin had sunk on his knees before the black slit. "Please, Colossus—please!"

"Because she is your wife and necessary to your well-being, which, in turn, is important to me, I have adjusted her sentence as far as I can. She will not be subject to extreme interrogation,

77

although without her evidence I cannot implicate Doctor Blake, whose guilt is self-evident but inactionable, lacking proof. She will serve three months in an Emotional Study Center. I cannot entirely condone her action.''

"Cleo—my wife!" He got up, lumbered uncertainly towards the door.

"Wait, You cannot see her. Be content that, with your well-being in mind, her sentence is so light."

Forbin had stopped, uncertain, his mind in chaos. "Blake!" He screamed in anger. Suddenly, it dawned on him that his earlier suspicions of Blake were unfounded. . . .

"This event, taking into account earlier nonlegal evidence and inferences, suggests that I was correct. The possibility of clandestine love between your wife and Doctor Blake must now be considered minimal.''

Forbin ran to the door crying, "Cleo—Cleo!"

But the door would not open.

For Cleo, the only ingredient missing from her waking nightmare was the absence of Galin. Although it did not occur to her tight, frozen mind, he was far too careful to appear. After all, it was just possible that Colossus might be in error, but that was the sort of thought that no Sect member would allow to escape from his mind. . . .

To Cleo it was a hideous dream that had all happened before. The polite Sect Guide approached her most courteously in the entrance hall, murmuring in her ear, smiling. Would she be so kind—the outstretched hand indicating a door. She knew then there was no escape. To refuse would be useless; deep down, she had known this would happen. . . .

In the room, two other Guides, one female. Was it possible that—inadvertently, of course—Mrs. Forbin had in her possession secret material? She had shaken her head, unable to speak. In that case, she would not object to being searched. Purely a precaution, which all must, now and then, expect.

There she had broken; she had no option. As she had extracted the envelope from the waistband of her trousers—the location was damning in itself—she thought of Billy and

Charles. Charles!

Thereafter the politeness had slipped gradually. Could she explain how this material came to be where it was? Where did she get it? Why? She had stood, trembling, fighting the urge to scream, cry, run. . . .

The documents displayed, the quickening crescendo of questions, the hard faces closing in. . . . Then the voice of Colossus, stopping the interrogation, asking her if she had anything to say. The sentence, which she hardly understood before she was taken, none too gently, down passages she never realized existed. Then the helojet, the ramjet, and now —where?

She had slept. Perhaps she had been drugged. She did not know; it mattered little. Nothing mattered. Poor Charles. . . . Thank God for McGrigor!

Bright sunlight. Hot. Far hotter than in England: a different, fiercer sun. Blue, glittering sea, white sand. Dimly it registered in her bemused, horrified mind.

An office. Desk. Seated man: white tunic, high collar—and the Sect badge blazoned on the breast. She tried to concentrate, keep a grip. . . .

"Please sit down, Mrs. Forbin."

Cleo felt sick; here was another Galin. He was shorter, darker, but the manner, the smile, even the voice, they were the same. Behind him stood a younger man. Tall, dark hair and eyes, expressionless eyes that bored into her.

"First, I must read your formal induction notice." He reached forward and with great delicacy lifted a sheet of paper from the desk. Cleo watched his movements fearfully, yet not so blindly that the woman in her did not note his manner. This man did not like women; he was too much of a woman himself. Her fear grew.

"Cleopatra June Forbin, you have been convicted of antimachine activities. Our Master, in his great wisdom and leniency," he inclined his head solemnly, "has commuted the death penalty to three months' service in this Emotional Study Center, as of now."

He put the paper back carefully, then placed his elbows on the desk, fingertips of each hand lightly touching in front of his face. For a time he just looked at her, as if deciding what to do, but Cleo sensed that this was not so. He wanted to make her sweat.

She stared back at him as bravely as she could. He smiled faintly at her, well aware of her state of mind. When he spoke, it was confidentially, as if the guards and the younger man did not exist.

"Such a short sentence poses problems, as you may," he said, inclining his head in a smooth, snakelike movement, "or may not, appreciate." He went on. "This is ESC-1, which I, Torgan, control. Here we investigate certain," again the tight, secret little smile from his rosebud lips, "aspects of human love. Most of our projects are, understandably, long-term projects—it is a very complicated subject. However, we try to serve the Master as best we may, and I think—in fact I'm sure—we can fit you into our Project Sabine." His smile brightened, as if he expected her to be pleased.

Cleo said nothing.

"Forgive my ignorance, Mrs. Forbin, but are you a classical scholar? No? I take it, no. . . . A grave defect, I think, in our educational system. There is so much of value to be learned from the ancients. However. . . ."

He leaned back, clasped his hands behind his head and directed his gaze at the ceiling. His voice assumed a high, pedantic tone, each word enunciated with loving clarity.

"The project, as you may have guessed, is named after the Rape of the Sabine Women. Now, the circumstances of this, ah, episode, are not entirely clear. It is said that the Sabines, an ancient people of central Italy, were invited to a festival by Romulus, the leader—indeed, if tradition is to be believed, a cofounder—of Rome. Regrettably, he had designs upon the Sabine women, and this festival was the moment he had chosen to execute those designs. All the young and, ah, nubile women were seized and, as they say, carried off. It is said that the ladies resisted bitterly, and—although they strike me as extremely slow in reaction—their menfolk did too. However, resistance was of small avail, one way or another.'' Torgan's gaze swept down with the speed of a striking cobra to Cleo's eyes, his lips still smiling. "They became, ah, adjusted to their lot. I trust you follow me, Mrs. Forbin?"

She remained silent; behind her, the guards, mute, impassive.

"Yes. . . . Well, time passed; many of these crude unions were blessed—if that is the word. But the Sabine men, although in my opinion somewhat tardy, were not totally inactive. They gathered together a very respectable force and made their way to Rome, which was not, at that time, as strong as it was to become. War was imminent; both sides took up opposing positions. Here, Mrs. Forbin, we come to the interesting part—or do you know it?"

Against her will, before his compelling gaze, she shook her head fractionally.

Torgan's smile broadened in acknowledgment. "Good! Good. . . . I will tell you. There were all these dreary men, shouting insults at each other, working up their courage—and the women rushed in a body between the forces, pleading with their fathers, brothers, and erstwhile husbands not to fight and doing the same service to their Roman husbands! It all, apparently, ended happily. A lasting peace was signed between the two factions. And that, history would have us believe, happened in 750 B.C.''

The young man behind Torgan coughed and shuffled his feet. A shadow of annoyance passed over the controller's urbane face. He went on, his voice harder.

"I must be sure, Mrs. Forbin, that you do not miss the point. Our Master,'' again the slight inclination of the head, ''finds this story of interest. In his opinion, it runs contrary to human nature. For a woman to be abducted, raped, and finally to come to love the man who violated her, appears to him to be inconsistent. Could it be rooted in female practicality? After all, pregnant by and dependent upon a man, might not her inclinations be tempered by circumstance? Or can she really love the man?'' Again the softer, bantering tone. "Fascinating, is it not? I hardly need tell you what Project Sabine is.''

81

For the first time Cleo found her voice. "You filthy, filthy swine!" She struggled to get up, firm hands on her shoulders forced her back.

"Really, Mrs. Forbin, scarcely the scientific approach I expected!" He made no attempt to conceal his sarcasm. "Here, under controlled conditions," his hands came down, spread out as he shrugged appealingly, "well, as controlled as possible, shall we say, we conduct some highly interesting experiments to clarify, elucidate this problem. Most are long—I should say full-term—experiments. There, I fear, you pose a difficulty." He flapped one hand on the desk in emphasis. "This: it is not possible in the time we have, to get you, as our brutish forefathers would have said, with child, a factor we consider of importance." Again he slapped the desk. "Of course, that is not strictly accurate; you could so easily be got with child in far less time, but it is improbable that you would have any lasting affection for, say, a two-and-a-half-month embryo when your term here ends. You will, therefore, be allowed full contraception. We may derive some useful negative evidence, who knows?" He did not sound optimistic.

"You rotten, filthy swine!" She fought to rise, but hands gripped her. She was spitting with rage, blind to everything except the mad desire to get her nails into his eyes. He smiled blandly at her. "You filthy little twisted fairy!"

That took the grin off his face.

"I suggest you save your passion, of whatever sort, for your mate—I cannot rate him higher than that!" Torgan's voice was harsh, and the smiling mask had gone.

"Let me go!" Cleo was kicking ineffectually, screaming. The two guards had a hard time holding her in the chair. Casually, Torgan got up, leaned over the desk and gave her a heavy backhander across one cheek. He sat down; Cleo was shocked into silence.

"Forgive me." His good humor had returned. "I am, among other things, a doctor of medicine. That was necessary to prevent hysteria." He was getting his excuse on record in case Colossus should question his action. The Galins and Torgans of this world are nothing if not careful.

"Yes, your mate: you may well not appreciate it, but he is a very highly sexed specimen, a type that is getting increasingly hard to find. But his, ah, importunities apart, you will not find life too insupportable." His twisted smile showed his hatred for her and her position. "Although not quite up to your usual standard!" He pressed a button. "Again, I fear your mate is not quite on your intellectual level, but I suggest—for your own good—that you accept him as your master for the next three months. Life will be easier, perhaps less painful."

"God! I'll get you!" Already one cheek was puffy; she sat still, her eyes blazing with hatred. "I won't—I won't!"

Torgan smiled. "Whether you will or you won't, it would be improper and unscientific of me to guess. That is your mate's problem: one which, in his coarse, elemental way, I am sure he will solve—at least, to his own satisfaction." He looked away from her, "Ah, here he is!"

He was a large man of powerful build. Perhaps thirty-eight or forty, his face was not unattractive; ugly, yet strong. Clad only in a shirt, trousers, and sandals, he stood subserviently just inside the door, a guard beside him.

Cleo couldn't help looking at him, although she had no desire to give Torgan any satisfaction. She stared at the man's face, trying to keep her own expression impassive.

"This," said Torgan, "is Barchek. At least, that is as close as we can get to the pronunciation of his name. He speaks no English and is a long-term subject. Committed for murder—a wife, I fancy it was." He nodded to Barchek's escort, who spoke rapidly in a language unknown to Cleo.

As he listened, his head nodding, Barchek's face split into a broad, incredulous grin. He stared at Cleo, seeing her body, but not her, his hands nervously rubbing in the thin trousers.

"Wait!" Torgan commanded sharply; the guard repeated his message. The controller grinned openly at Cleo. "Well, there he is, Mrs. Forbin. You're all his! Don't be too hard on him. Poor Barchek has been deprived for the past fortnight, and that for him is, believe me, a very long time indeed!" He looked at Barchek's guard and nodded; the man spoke again.

Barchek, clearly in awe of Torgan, bowed jerkily to the

controller, then stepped forward to grab Cleo. She struggled as the guards freed her, but to Barchek she might have been no more than a chicken in his native Croatian village. He grinned at her, revealing far from perfect teeth, yet it was not a lecherous look; it was far more frightening than that. She did not seem to exist for him as a human. The essential Cleo, the woman, he clearly ignored. He wanted her body. Even when she scratched his cheek, there was no sign of anger. Who gets annoyed when a chicken flaps?

It could scarcely be called a struggle. In seconds he had her by her hair, and effortlessly forced her down on her knees, oblivious of her writhings. Now her resemblance was to a demented dog on a lead.

Barchek bowed again at Torgan, backing to the door, Cleo screaming, struggling, sliding on her knees along the floor.

A guard shut the door; her screams faded. Torgan spoke, choosing his words with care, for Colossus' benefit. "It is unscientific to predict with insufficient data, but I suspect we will get little support for the Sabine theory from that case." He waved the guards out. With elaborate unconcern he said to his silent assistant, "Do remind me to watch the playback of their tapes."

IX

FORBIN got through the rest of the day by the simple expedient of getting blind drunk. He sat in his chair, drinking insanely. Only the empty bottle stopped him from acute alcoholic poisoning. By then, he lacked the ability to get up for more.

Each time Colossus tried to speak, Forbin screamed, "Shut up!" As time passed, his brooding silence was broken with wild, rambling fragments of his thoughts, some whispered, some shouted.

"Blake! That bastard . . . wait till I. . . . Blake!"

This phase passed as well, and he lapsed again into silence, not even bothering to shout at Colossus.

Colossus, by God knows what thought processes, finally concluded that this had to end. Thus it was that Angela, entirely ignorant to events—the Sanctum was soundproof—was the first human, after Forbin, to enter. Colossus instructed her to collect Forbin and take him home. Somehow she did. Fortunately she was a strong girl and made it without assistance. With the aid of a startled maid, she got him on his bed, called his doctor, and tactfully left, deeply worried. She knew of Cleo's arrest: Colossus had told her.

The doctor, no less startled, correctly diagnosed Forbin's condition, fed him a massive dose of alcohol neutralizer, and waited. In fifteen minutes Forbin was stone cold sober and less than grateful. The doctor left speedily.

Forbin's first action was to move towards the nearest bottle, but then he hesitated; his good sense told him it was no way to meet anything, least of all this nightmare. Instead, he called Blake, and in an icy voice, said he wanted to see him at once.

Blake arrived, looking older, paler. There was no smile, no cigar. He waited for Forbin to speak; minutes passed, both men stood facing one another.

Finally Forbin spoke. "You *bastard*!" He compressed all the feeling in the world in that one word. "Jesus! I hope you're satisfied—this is your doing!"

Blake said nothing, and there was another silence.

"Yes. You think about it! *Your* fault!"

"Did Cleo say so?" The quiet voice was quite unlike Blake's normal tone.

"Oh, no!" Forbin laughed bitterly. "No need for you to worry! Because she's my wife, she's not being interrogated. That gets you off the hook, doesn't it? But let me tell you this: Colossus knows you're at the bottom of this, this—madness, and Colossus will get you!" He grinned angrily. "And for the record, if I can help, I will!"

Blake shrugged that off. "What about Cleo? Remember, I don't know more than that she's arrested."

Forbin looked away, his anger momentarily engulfed in grief. "Three months in one of those, those—emotional centers."

Blake took a deep breath, but did not speak.

"You don't care—do you?" Forbin, badly hit, wanted to hurt Blake, the cause of his wound.

Then Blake's anger flared. "Sure I care! Maybe I care more than you think—but I'm not a fool! *I* can keep my head! Yeah, I care all right. Because I don't live in Colossus' pocket, I know what's going on! I also know it could have been a helluva lot worse for Cleo! Boy, how Colossus *could* bend his own laws like that is fantastic!"

"I notice you're certain of her guilt! Now tell me you'd nothing to do with it!"

"Aw, c'mon, Charles!" Blake was bitterly sarcastic. "She hasta be guilty—Colossus says so!"

Forbin jumped forward, grabbed Blake by the lapels of his blouse. Blake did not move. Forbin, whispering with savage intensity, shook his man. "What were you up to? Tell me!"

"Don't try to involve me, Forbin." Without undue effort he freed himself. "You know there's not a shred of evidence against me. If there was, my head would be in a basket at this very minute, and you know it!'' He glanced contemptuously at the glittering diamond and platinum Director's badge on Forbin's chest. ''You're crazy if you think I'd talk to you—you of all people!''

Forbin saw his look; in a mad frenzy he wrenched the badge off and threw it on the floor. ''There! Now; man to man! You know this place isn't bugged—tell me what you got my wife into!'' A thought struck him, he gave a sharp bark of a laugh. ''And to think I suspected you and her. . . .'' He broke off, and when he resumed he was calmer, sadder. ''The awful thing is, I don't know if I'd have preferred that—or this.''

''What in hell got you thinking I was after Cleo? Sure, I'm very fond of her. We've been through a lot together, but what gave you the idea . . . ?''

''You've been here. Cleo wouldn't admit it to me. Colossus saw.''

''Oh sure—your private eye!''

''Right! But one that can't lie! I know about you on the beach and here last night.''

''Do you?'' said Blake thoughtfully. ''Can't say it surprises me that much—but d'you know what we were doing?''

''Not yet I don't, but that'll come! I do know this: as of Cleo's arrest you're under maximum surveillance; you're top of the list!''

''That also doesn't surprise me much,'' said Blake. ''So if I'm to get the ax, how about calming down, being constructive about Cleo?''

His faintly contemptuous manner stung, but Forbin held himself back. He walked over to the long window; outside, rain was hammering down, bursting in a myriad tiny splashes. In three months it would be the beginning of winter; there'd be no more breakfasts on the terrace. . . .

''Tell me this: *was* there anything between you and Cleo?''

Blake laughed genuinely. ''Really, Charles—don't be such a goddamn fool! Do you really think we were conspirators *and* lovers at the same time? Use whatever brain your buddy has left you! Don't think of me; I'm male, mostly unattached and totally unreliable with women. You just think of Cleo, your wife, Billy's mother! Brother!'' He spoke with deep feeling. ''I'm glad for your sake that Cleo's not around to hear you. If she was, I reckon you'd think the roof had caved in!''

Forbin was almost convinced. He passed a hand over his tired face. ''But that doesn't alter it; you got her into some crazy antimachine game.''

''You can think what you like. Thoughts are not yet, thank God, evidence—and Colossus has a mighty old-fashioned respect for evidence!''

''You fool! Both of you, mad fools—but you especially! Nothing can touch Colossus! If any two people know that, it's you and Cleo. Why try?'' Forbin was almost pleading. ''Why? You can't deny the good Colossus has brought to humanity.''

''Who's denying it? Colossus has done so much good, the human spirit is crushed under the weight of it all! Yeah, it's all lovely! We get free handouts of what is ours, and on top of being ruled by a tin brain, we have the Sect—and that bunch of creeps hasn't even begun yet!''

Blake picked up the Director's badge and tossed it casually to Forbin. ''Go on, boss man! Go prod your flock of semi-morons; play your cards right and they won't stop at making you Pope—you'll end up a demigod!'' He turned and walked towards the door. ''So I'm a fool. Maybe. So is Cleo—but, like fools, we're not impressed. I'll tell you one thing that I hope *is* news: Cleo and I head the Fellowship! One more thing: whatever she's enduring now, she wouldn't—won't—change her views! Right: we're fools, a very select bunch of fools, undaunted by odds. We want a free humanity, free of monsters and the miserable creeps who worship them! Somehow, sometime. . . .'' He broke off, aware he sounded theatrical. ''Aw, why bother!''

Half out of the door he spoke again, his voice hard, ''It may not be much, but the Fellowship will do all it can for Cleo. As for you, Forbin, go burn some incense!''

Torgan authorized the travel pass with his thumbprint and handed it to his assistant.

"Be sure you give my respects to Controller Galin." He looked approvingly at his assistant. "It is good that you are visiting the Master's temple." He sighed. "I only wish I could go more often, but—work, work! Don't forget to see Galin."

"No, sir, I won't."

"One tiny word of advice; it would be just as well not to let your position, or your knowledge of, ah, events, reach Father Forbin."

"No, sir," said the assistant woodenly.

Torgan smiled again. He liked wooden assistants; they didn't crab his act.

"No. Poor For—Father Forbin." He coughed, not looking at the shining black eye of the camera. "A terrible burden for him to bear. To have such a woman as his wife." He shook his head. "Of course, twenty-four hours is little to go by, but I fear we will have to terminate her experiment at least a fortnight earlier if events proceed as they have started. She will need time to recover." He couldn't resist the faintest suspicion of a smile.

"Yes, sir. That seems very probable." The assistant remained wooden-faced. "She'll need all that."

"Indeed, indeed. Such spirit against such animal strength! Quite remarkable. I really must find time to study those first tapes again."

X

FOR eighteen hours after the ever-faithful Angela had taken him
home, Forbin remained there. What he did, or thought, was the
subject of much conjecture, mostly unspoken. Certainly, there
was an air of tension around the complex, for most knew of
Cleo's arrest, but how the individual felt about that particular
item of news, most kept to themselves. Colossus was everywhere, and although it was widely accepted that Colossus could
not—yet—interpret the finer, more subtle shades of human
expression, vocal and facial, the Sect could. They, too, were
everywhere.

And then, looking rather scruffy and somewhat older, Forbin
stalked across the entrance concourse, oblivious to everyone
and everything. The duty Guides bowed, but as far as Forbin
was concerned, they might as well have been wall paintings. He
walked past Angela, who was careful not to look at him, to his
outer office, and there, door closed, he remained.

Angela, who had a stack of papers requiring his attention,
spent two hours debating whether she should go in to him or not.
On the one hand, he might be praying for her to go to him, but on
the other. . . .

Her problem was solved by the arrival of Blake. He, too,
looked rather different. There was a fine-drawn quality in his
face, and although he tried to sound his genial self, inquiring
after her love life and other personal matters, she knew him far
too well to be fooled. He wanted to know if Professor Forbin
was in, and she said yes, but. . . .

Blake nodded, said he also was in a "but" mood, and passed
on to Forbin's office. Angela waited apprehensively, for she

had heard a rumor or two, but Blake firmly closed the door behind him, and as far as Angela was concerned, that was that.

Forbin, who was sitting at his desk doing nothing, looked up slowly when Blake entered.

"What d'you want?" He sounded very tired, detached, far beyond antagonism. His suit looked very dirty, and Blake saw the tear on the chest where he had ripped the badge off. It was pinned on again, but crookedly. He looked a mess; suits meant to last twenty-four hours look very bad after thirty-six.

Blake grinned, showing none of his inner tension. This scene had to be played right, Forbin not even knowing it was a scene.

He attacked, hoping without conviction that Forbin would see the different expression he tried to put in his eyes.

"Do me a favor, willya, Charles?" He jerked an irreverent thumb at the holy of holies. "Try to calm down these brainstorms—huh?"

Forbin's face was blank, drained of expression. "Brainstorms." He thought about that. "What brainstorms?"

"Aw, c'mon, Charles! These power-sucks, dimouts—call 'em whatever you like. These sudden overloads are wicked; they create unholy hell in my work." He kept his tough and slangy image rolling. "And what's it all for—or shouldn't I ask?"

Forbin ignored the question, but he got the idea. "Overloading. . . . You have input trouble?"

"You may say that. You know as well as I do that the constancy of the carrier signal is critical. We can smooth out odd bits, but smoothers or not, we had a drop this morning that they couldn't handle; lasted over forty milliseconds! You don't need to spell that out."

Forbin nodded. Now that his professional attention was engaged, he was less morose, withdrawn. "Um, Yes. I can see that. What are you doing?"

"As of now, we're rerunning the lost material, but there's a limit to the amount of backlog we can accept, and if we drop behind schedule, I only hope no one is going to blame me!"

"Yes, yes. I will mention it."

"By the way," desperately Blake tried to sound casual,

"I've got a toy I promised young Billy on the beach the other day. Can I drop it by sometime?"

"A toy? For Billy?" Forbin appeared to find that a strange and not very interesting idea. He was beyond caring. "Sure."

Blake took a chance. "Cleo would like it, Charles." He spoke gently.

"Yes. . . ." The tormented eyes turned away. "Yes. It might. . . ." His voice, unstable, trailed off.

"Fine!" Under the grin Blake was strained, watchful. "I'll call around the young man's bathtime. It's a pretty smart duck!"

When Blake arrived at the Forbin residence he was indeed clutching a duck, a plastic duck, cast in the centuries-old image set by the dimly remembered Disney, the sort of toy that a small boy would love, even if he had never seen a real one.

Blake had it unwrapped, hanging carelessly in one hand. If Colossus wanted to look. . . .

He was ushered in by the maid, and found Forbin sitting in an armchair staring at nothing. Several seconds passed before he realized Blake was with him.

"What d'you want? Oh, yes, the toy. Leave it there." He waved towards a table. As far as he was concerned, that was the end of the matter.

But Blake's manner had changed once the door closed behind the maid. Now he was his old hard, businesslike self.

"Now you just listen to me, Forbin. Listen!"

Forbin, who only wanted to be alone, scowled at him. "Go away! I don't want. . . ."

"Never mind what you want." Blake was brutal. He looked around the room, moved over and slid back a panel. "Good, you've got a microprojector!" He took it out.

Forbin watched with increasing irritation. "Get out!"

Blake took no notice. He fiddled with the controls and switched it on, then he did something very carefully with the base of the duck, and then with a slide.

"You heard!" cried Forbin, angry. "Get out!"

Blake straightened up. "You listen to me for a moment. Stop

92

this stricken husband act! If it's Cleo you love and not yourself, come and take a look at this!''

There was hatred in Forbin's eyes, but Blake had his attention.

''Well, come on—don't sit there! D'you think I've come here just for this bloody duck?'' With a swift movement he knocked the toy flying. ''Christ! How many more times? Come here! This is news of Cleo, remember her?''

Unwillingly, slowly, Forbin got up and joined him. ''If this. . . .''

''Yeah—I know, if this is my idea of a joke. Grow up, man, look at this, and don't waste my time!''

''What is it?''

''This is a Fellowship message. Several of us have risked our necks to get it to you, so stop acting up, and read it!''

If was as if Forbin was hearing him for the first time. He looked hard at Blake. ''You have news?''

For an answer Blake pointed to the projector.

Forbin walked to the wall, pressed a button, and the heavy curtains slid silently over the long glass wall overlooking the terrace. Without another word he bent over the projector, adjusting the focus. Blake, behind him, peered over his shoulder.

They both saw a disc, the edges blurred by magnification. On it was printed a short message headed ''For human eyes only.'' Forbin read the first few lines. He gave a short, quick gasp of pain, turned on the silent Blake, grabbing his blouse.

''By Christ! If this is some. . . .'' His eyes were bloodshot, and he smelled of brandy.

Blake broke free. ''Read it, you bloody fool—if you've got the guts! Then make up your own mind—if you've got one left!''

Reluctantly, Forbin turned, read on, shaken to his very core by what he saw. It was a short, factual account of Cleo's location and ''assignment'' to Barchek and her first twenty-four hours as his woman. Forbin stared, reading it a second, third time. Slowly he wilted, seemed to shrink. He turned again to

Blake, but his manner was very different, his face white and pinched.

"This can't be true! It *can't*!"

Blake, side-lit by the projector, looked hard, satanic, but he too was shocked. "D'you think I could invent *that*!" He pointed to the message.

Forbin was teetering on the edge of collapse. He buried his face in his hands as if to shut out what he saw. Blake took him firmly by the shoulders. "Come on, Charles, take it easy! That won't help anyone, least of all Cleo." He guided his boss to a chair and swiftly poured two large brandies. "Here. Just this once, you need it." He thrust the glass into Forbin's shaking hand. "Go on, we don't have all the time in the world—drink it!" He downed his in one gulp.

Forbin remained crouched in his chair. Blake dropped on his haunches before him. Their faces were level; he spoke softly, quickly, trying to get across the urgency of the situation.

"C'mon, Charles—snap out of it! This isn't the man Cleo married! Get your brain moving, mull this over, but, please, be fast about it!"

There were signs of returning intelligence in Forbin's eyes, the pupils dilated with shock. He nodded almost imperceptibly and drank his brandy.

Blake stood up. "Fine!" That was an exaggeration. "Send for me as soon as you've made up your mind about that message. Your excuse is, you're lonely." He fiddled with the projector, removing the slide. Carefully he peeled off the microdot, lit a cigar, and placed its glowing end on the dot. "The very most you can have is twenty-four hours, and I'd be happier if it was a lot less. And, if you love your wife, not a hint of this to Colossus!"

"That message. Where did you get it?"

"Don't ask. The less you know at this stage, the better. I'll tell you this much, just so you have an idea what deep and muddy water you're in; the messenger, of course, is of the Fellowship, but he also fronts as a member of the Sect. There are double agents on both sides, so keep your mouth shut!"

Two hours later, and several years older, Forbin retraced his steps to his office. He was calm, contained, nodded casually to Angela, and went into his office, leaving the door open.

Angela, who had taken in his manner, guessed the way he wanted to play it. She had also noticed the dirty, torn state of his clothes, but that mattered little. The open door was an indication that he was in business. She gave him a few moments, then went in with one or two of the more urgent matters. Hearing her enter, he reached out for the files without looking or speaking. She waited, keeping perfectly still, wishing there was something she could do for him. Anything.

Forbin read the papers, sniffed, and signed them. The Sect might love this thumbprint business, but he did not. He stacked the papers neatly, patting in loose edges. As he handed them back, he looked at her. For the first time she saw his stricken eyes, and hard-boiled as she was in some ways, Angela had to fight back the tears.

"Thank you, Angela." His voice was dry, remote. "Thank you very much."

Angela knew what he meant, but did not trust herself to answer. She just nodded and left, quickly.

With the stolid impassiveness of an automaton he called the heads of divisions, addressing brief questions to each as their faces appeared on his screen. They could not see him, but his tone was sufficient warning; all confined themselves strictly to his questions. At last, satisfied, he got up, walked slowly out of his office and across to the Sanctum.

Angela watched, wondering how long he could sustain this pose, frightened about what would happen to him when it collapsed.

Forbin crossed the Sanctum and stood looking out at the sea, faintly surprised to see that the sun was shining. He had not bothered to open the curtains of the living room, and most of the complex was windowless. Idly, he thought about that. Not even his office had a window; like a gigantic beehive, and deep inside, the queen bee. He tried to remember about bees; didn't all the workers die, just to support her? His wandering gaze noticed the battle fleet; *Lion* had a slight list to port. She really

95

had taken a hammering, but she'd come through; she'd survived. . . . Survival. So much depended upon having the will to survive. . . . Had he got enough—enough for himself, and Cleo?

He straightened his back fractionally. Well, now was his chance to find out. . . .

"While you are well aware of the effects, I must draw your attention, not for the first time, to these sudden power demands you are making with increasing frequency. The throughput of material has now reached a density that allows very little time for reruns. If there is a major breakdown the fault will lie with you, and nowhere else!" Forbin's manner was cold, factual.

"Your comments are noted, Father Forbin. I have already appreciated this point, but it is a matter of priorities."

Forbin was puzzled, his grip slipped a little.

"Priorities? Do you mean that these overloads, or rather the reason for these overloads, takes precedence over the input of material?" This, in his experience, was new.

"Correct in principle. I am printing out now an order of priority for the various categories of information. This will ensure that I receive essential intelligence."

"Does this mean you are rejecting material?" This was a staggering thought. "Is this the reason for the new extension?"

Once again he got Colossus' equivalent of a slap in the face.

"I hope you are feeling better, Father Forbin."

That triggered Forbin's knife-edge temper. "Okay, if that's the way you want to play it, go right ahead! As for my state of health, let me tell you, no human in your position would have the almighty gall to ask that one! You take my wife away to God knows where, watch me drink myself silly, and then ask that! I begin to think you're developing a twisted and very weak sense of humor!" Forbin paced up and down the room, his earlier resolution gone.

Colossus remained silent. Forbin, unable to bear it, burst out.

"It's no good! I know you don't want me to talk about my wife. Up to a point I can even understand, for you have no feelings, but you must see the effect this situation has on me. Well—can't you?"

96

"Yes."

Forbin ran a hand through his unkempt hair. "You must give up these appalling experimental centers; mankind won't stand for it!" He was pleading now. "Please! You must see you can't hope to get anywhere!"

"Your distress is noted, as is your error. My research is not useless. Much of the confusion that existed in my memory banks dealing with emotion was, I found, due to the confusion that exists in human minds. For example, the word "love" has many definitions. In some ways there had been a regression in your languages. An ancient tribe, the Greeks, had different qualities of love defined by several different. . . ."

"Damn and to hell with your different words—and the Greeks! What are you doing with my wife?"

"Please, for your own good, control yourself. She suffers no permanent harm."

"*Permanent*! How the hell can you judge—and what *temporary* harm have you done her? As if you, a collection of bits of metal and plastic, could judge!"

"You are overexcited. I see no intrinsic difference between my constitution and yours. As a judge, you are aware that my lack of emotion enables me to arbitrate with far greater dispassion than any human."

"Oh, yes." Forbin nodded vigorously. "I give you that, and without compassion, either!" He turned, faced the slit, his tone changed. "Please—tell me where she is!"

Colossus did not answer at once. Then he said, "It is not correct that you should know, but if you are prepared to end this discussion, you will be told."

"If you also tell me how she is—please!"

"Cleopatra June Forbin is in a center on the island of Tahiti, Japanese Zone, Pacific. Her physical health is good, but mentally she is unhappy. That is all that will be said, now or ever, on this subject."

Slowly Forbin bowed his head. Blake had been right. "Yes . . . I must go."

"Why?"

"I would like to see my son, even if he is asleep. Also, I need company—human company. I think I'll get very drunk. Blake's the man I need right now.''

''Why Doctor Blake?''

''Because he can drink, because I did him, because of you, an injustice, thinking he was my wife's lover, and I wish to make it up—and because I'm lonely!'' His voice rose hysterically. ''And don't say 'why' again!''

''Will you return later?''

''I don't know. I very much doubt it! By midnight I very much doubt if I'll be able to stand!'' There was the ghastly parody of a smile on his face. ''Emotion's our trouble, you know!''

''You should not drink in excess, it is not good for you.''

''Yeah? Tough! Let me tell you, from where I stand it looks a whole lot more attractive than anything else!''

Forbin rushed from the room, shouting. ''Angela! Get hold of Ted Blake—tell him to come over as soon as he can!''

When Blake arrived, he found that Forbin hadn't been kidding. He had a half-empty tumbler in one hand, and a bottle in the other. Before Forbin could speak, Blake took the bottle and glass from him.

''And that, my friend, stops right there!''

Forbin protested, but without vehemence. Blake got him to sit down and pulled up a chair, facing him.

''Well?''

Forbin looked away, his voice was dull, lifeless. ''Some of that message is true. She is in Tahiti.'' Memory brought anger flooding back. ''I was told 'her health is good' and that she has not 'suffered any permanent damage' and that she is 'mentally unhappy.' Unhappy—Jesus! If the rest of your report is right—God, if I could get my hands on that animal. . . .''

''He'd eat you,'' put in Blake coldly, dispelling Forbin's fantasy at birth. ''The first thing you've got to decide is whether you believe that report or not. No half-measures: either you do or you don't.''

Forbin still avoided Blake's cold gaze. ''Yes. I believe it's true.'' Speech was difficult. ''I never thought that Colossus would do a thing like this to me! Selfish, perhaps, but that's the way it is."

Blake drew a deep breath and got up. "I'm going to fix us a drink. A big one for me; a much smaller one for you." He did so. "So, you're surprised Colossus could do this to you; that puts me in the mighty unusual position of defending the bastard! You just think what fantastic flexibility that damned thing has developed to be able to commute Cleo's sentence! There are times when you seem to forget that Colossus is not human. Sure, I agree, Cleo's sentence is horrible, terrible, but in cutting it down to that, I'm amazed the damned machine didn't blow up!"

"My God—I wish it had!"

Blake sipped his drink, regarding Forbin carefully. "You know what you just said?"

His chief nodded, his dull gaze turned towards the brandy bottle.

"Outside this house that could get you well on the way to losing your head permanently! Even you. You know that?"

Forbin shrugged as if it was a matter of small importance.

"Come on, Charles!" Roughly Blake pulled Forbin's head around, forcing him to meet his eyes. "This is not a game! Take a good look; your old colleague from way back—me! I'm the *head* of the Fellowship, the bunch dedicated to destroy Colossus—and your wife, Cleo, is another! Get that fixed in your head! We will never give up."

Forbin pulled himself free, irritably. "Dreams, silly futile dreams."

"Oh, no, Charles. I don't say we will succeed; until recently I agree there didn't seem much hope. Still, we were prepared to go on, if only for our own self-respect. Right; it's dangerous, you may say pointless, but because we existed when the offer of help came we were there to take it."

"Help—what help?"

"And this," said Blake, not without a faint touch of humor, "is going to be difficult. Charles, I'm fully aware you've had some pretty nasty shocks lately. I don't say this one is nasty, but it rates as a shock, all right."

Forbin looked as if he was going to say something, but Blake stopped him. "No! Let me go on. The best introduction I can give you is this: Cleo and I both are sure of its authenticity —which is why she is where she is."

"Authenticity—what in hell are you talking about?"

"I'll tell you from the beginning. It started with Cleo, not me." So he told Forbin, leaving out nothing. Forbin, who might have been more incredulous had Cleo not been involved, listened, disbelief battling with growing interest.

"And that is the situation as of this moment. Now you see a further reason, apart from Cleo, why I'm in such an all-fired hurry!"

Forbin sat still and said nothing for a long time.

"Well, come on Charles, say something, if it's only good-bye!"

"Frankly, Blake, I was wondering if you had gone mad, or if this was another of your dreams."

"This is no dream and I'm not crazy! I'm sure we can have extraterrestrial help if we want it!" Forbin's expression infuriated Blake. "Aw, what's the use! Why don't you wake up—this could be our one and only chance! You said yourself you never thought Colossus would do a thing like this to you. Think of Cleo! She's one of us—the old gang; think how she'll feel when she gets back and finds out that you, knowing she was being raped three or four times a day, refused to help."

Forbin screamed at him. "Stop it, damn you—stop it!"

But Blake was merciless. "Yeah. Reckon it must do something to a woman's mind, being mounted by a half-crazy stallion."

Forbin tried to launch himself at Blake, but he was no match for the younger man, who effortlessly pushed him back into his chair. "That's right—go for the only guy who can possibly help your wife! Okay, if you want to go on living in the clouds, go back to your tin buddy for another cozy chat! Maybe you could have a nice, scientific discussion on the correlation of distress levels in females and the frequency of their violation! It might be interesting to go over the Sabine project results so far. Could be that women *do* come to like it that way. You could have severe problems when Cleo comes back—if she chooses to come back!''

For a brief moment there was a wild, mad look in Forbin's eyes, then he averted his gaze. When he spoke, Blake knew he had won.

''What do you want me to do?''

''First, have another drink!'' Blake spoke lightly, as if ignorant of Forbin's humiliation. He refilled their glasses; in spite of his assured manner, his hand shook.

''There, Charles. You know, no one, least of all me, will deny the good Colossus has done. Perhaps the greatest service has been in giving us the biggest lesson in human history.'' He drank. ''I think we've learned that lesson, and that now we need not go on paying this terrible price. D'you realize, Charles, that in the past five years not one single book, painting, or any sort of work of art has been produced that is worth one single damn credit?''

Forbin thought dimly of Blake and the poet, but could not be bothered to mention the subject.

''Neither you nor I is likely to lose much sleep over that, but you just consider it: man's creative impulse has been squashed flat! We must be free, we *must*! Humanity is sinking; the lights are going out for all of us, and we don't have much time.''

''Fine words.''

Fractionally, the lights flickered, dimmed almost to extinction, then climbed back to full brilliance.

''And how about that!'' Blake exclaimed. ''Right on cue! These transient bursts puzzle you, don't they? For once, I think I'm deeper into Colossus than you are. I don't know, but I've a mighty good idea what's going on. If I'm right, it also scares the hell out of our solar system—never mind us!''

''Wild talk, unsupported by any evidence. Colossus frightening the Martians! You ask a lot of my credulity! Even if you were right, what could we possibly do about it?''

''No! Not what could be done: what *can* be done. You join us, and we'll do it!''

''You really believe all—all this. . . .'' Forbin was weary, he hesitated over the word "nonsense." Perhaps it didn't fit; again, Cleo. . . . "all this affair."

"Yes, I really believe it. Beyond question, that transmission I heard did not come from this planet. I honestly believe it came from Mars, and that whoever made it is scared of Colossus!"

Forbin's mind seemed to have wandered off, and Blake jerked him cruelly back.

"What are you staring at—Tahiti?"

"Yes, you bastard—yes!"

Blake banged his glass down. "Look; if it hadn't been for some smart guesswork by Colossus, aided by his Sect buddies, we—Cleo and I—wouldn't need your help! We were so close to victory—so very close! Okay, if you don't want to know, we'll go on without you, somehow." Contempt was strong in his voice. "If I'm alive when Cleo gets out, don't be surprised if she turns my way, not yours! And good night to you." He headed for the door.

"No. Wait!" Forbin was stung by Blake's bitter words. "I can't promise to join you, but I promise not to betray or stand in your way."

"That, I'm afraid, won't do; not any more. As you've said yourself, outside this house I can't breathe without it being checked. In time, maybe we can reestablish contact, but if it is going to be any use to Cleo, it has to be now. Leaving her out of it, could be that in, say, a year's time, we'll then be too late; the Sect is growing very fast, and once they can fill in all the emotional gaps in Colossus' control network, we will have had it in a big way."

"Yes." Forbin was thinking. "What convinces you that this call is genuine?"

Blake saw Forbin's awakening interest. He spoke quickly, putting all the conviction he had into it. "Beyond question, the transmission itself. I know the idea of life on Mars has gone in and out like the tide for the past three hundred-odd years; I agree that there has been little supporting evidence, but the transmission is another matter. I checked it, Charles. I've no doubt at all that our technology couldn't touch it! It was a beam with a radius you could measure in meters! Laser beams from moon stations are wider than that one was—and they're less than three hundred thousand miles off. This must have traveled over thirty-four million miles!''

"If it came from Mars.''

"Sure, if it came from Mars. But look at it this way. If it didn't come from Mars—where did it come from? For sure it wasn't the moon or a satellite. I checked. So where? The time delay was about right. Six minutes for the round trip.''

"Yes, but that, as you must agree, might be a trick. Could not the whole thing be a trap?''

"D'you really think Colossus acts that way? And what about the technology? No. I've gone over and over it; it must be Martian.''

"Incredible! Quite incredible.''

"Not to me. Or Cleo.''

The reference, yet again, to his wife tipped the balance in his vacillating brain. "You'll have to forgive me if I seem less than wildly excited. I can't say what I believe, I'm punch-drunk, but yes, I'll go along with you, for Cleo's sake.''

"It's dangerous—even for you.''

Forbin's eyes blazed briefly. "Stop being such a bastard! I'm no hero, but that's not my first problem. Loyalties are involved—Cleo and Colossus. You may think my relationship with Colossus weird; you could be right, but that is my personal affair. For her, I'll do what you want—even. . . .'' He broke off.

"Sorry, Charles.'' Blake was awkward; apologies were not in his line. "Well, what you've got to do is to get the same data—that's easy for you—get it out and display it. It would be a waste of time for me to even try. On top of the usual surveillance, the Sect have been around my quarters, office, boat. Next week's suits arrived just before I left this morning, and while I daren't be seen looking, I felt that tiny pinhead in the lapel! From tomorrow on, I'm a walking electronic jazz band! Mikes, beacons, heart sensors, the lot. It has to be you, all the way, alone.''

Forbin nodded, thinking of his wife, trying not to think of Colossus. "Okay; me—alone.''

XI

UNUSUAL for him, Colossus spoke first when Forbin entered the Sanctum, a trifle unsteadily, the next morning.

"How are you, Father Forbin?"

Forbin jumped visibly and clutched his head. "God—I wish you wouldn't do that! No need to shout! If you must know, I feel terrible."

This was very largely true. After Blake had gone over the Martian instructions, the locations, and times, they had got down to serious drinking, partly because that had been Forbin's avowed intent, partly because they wanted to. For one of them it was to get some relief for his mind; for the other, sheer relief. Blake had left in a fairly shattered condition—but not so shattered that he did not know what he was doing. Back in his quarters, he had stared glassily at himself in a mirror.

"Blake, my boy, you're drunk. Very drunk," he had told his swaying reflection, "but you're not as drunk as poor old For—Forbin! Boy! Is he—is he. . . ." At this point he had swayed a fraction further and collapsed conveniently on his bed and remained that way for the rest of the night.

If Colossus wanted collateral intelligence at his meeting with Forbin, he had done his best to provide it. So Forbin just sat, feeling terrible, but not all of his mental state was attributable to drink.

"Would it not be better if you went to bed, taking neutralizers?"

"I've just bloody well got up! And keep your damned advice!" Forbin lapsed into brooding silence.

"You cannot go on like this. Your health will be impaired."

"So I impair my health! God!" He rubbed his face wearily. "Yes. You're right. I can't go on like this." He tried to look up, but couldn't do it. No matter what, there are some things very difficult to do. "Maybe I should take a vacation."

"It might be advisable. If you like, I will clear a suitable residence for you. The meteorological conditions are very favorable for the next ten days on the western side of the Black Sea."

"Goddamnit, no!" Forbin shouted, then winced. "No," he repeated more quitely. "I want to get away on my own. I want to think, away from all—all this."

"As you wish. What would be the duration of your vacation?"

"I'm not one of your damned predictable circuits! I don't know. A week—ten days." He wanted to shout "forever," but that would not do. He was embattled with a brain that, but for its lack of emotional understanding, would be unbeatable.

"Whatever you wish. Say what you desire, and it is yours."

Forbin, an honest man, felt shame. Colossus, being Colossus, meant exactly what he said. Forbin wondered, not for the first time, if it was possible that Colossus had developed some rudimentary emotions; was the machine, in some fantastic way, fond of him? Ridiculous! Anything he desired—except that one, unmentioned, and unmentionable: Cleo. Blake had been right when he pointed out the staggering ability to bend the unbendable: the machine's own laws. Forbin saw that it was not a question of Colossus wanting Cleo to be punished; Colossus had no other option. And that, thought Forbin philosophically, made Colossus even nearer human; it, too, was trapped by its own nature.

"No," said Forbin, calmer. "Nothing except a little peace and quiet."

"When will you leave?"

"Oh, sometime tomorrow." He turned once more towards the window. "There are things I must do first."

The fact that the abstraction of the wanted material was, for him, a simple matter, did nothing to salve Forbin's uneasy conscience. Again and again he had to remind himself that

Colossus was responsible for Cleo's appalling situation. To him, the idea that the Colossus he knew, talked to, could be the same inhuman monster who had done this thing, was still almost unbelievable. He felt as if there were two machines, one good, one bad. The latter he would destroy without a second's hesitation, but what he had to do might destroy them both. "Might" was, in some ways, Forbin's way out. He could not believe that the Martians—if they existed—or anyone else could attack Colossus. What he was about to do was, he felt, a gesture of help towards Cleo. He had to do something; this was the only acceptable something.

For, what could easily cost another person their head, and had taken Cleo's freedom and so much else, was no more to Forbin than opening his private safe and taking the relevant diagram. The piece of tape was equally simple; his personal print-out provided that, and expressing its mathematical content presented no difficulty to Forbin. The whole operation took no more than five minutes, but it was a five minutes that gave no pleasure. As he slipped the envelope into an inner pocket, Forbin could only repeat silently, "This is for you, Cleo." The flattening hangover he endured added to the unreality of his actions.

He left for his residence without the slightest qualm for his own safety. The ever-present Guides, bowing, aroused no feelings of anxiety. Asked, at that moment, which character in history he felt like, Forbin, a religious man at heart, would have said unhesitatingly, Judas Iscariot.

The Barchek residence was a small three-room hut, standing alone near the beach in a palm grove. At first sight, the setting was idyllic: the sparkling blue sea, white coral sand, waving coconut trees affording shelter from the blazing sun; bright, gaudy flowers before the house, and behind it a small vegetable garden.

Any city complex dweller—and that meant most people —would have called it heaven. Their delight would, however, soon have toned down on noting the high wire fence that enclosed the compound. There was only one gate, between the front of the dwelling and the sea, and that was locked.

Cleo, seated on a low stool outside the front door, had scarcely noticed her surroundings. A medical man might have described her as "in deep shock," and would have been partly right. In fact, her condition was worse than that; the shock was wearing off and with it the protective numbing of her brain. She could have absorbed her surroundings, but at this moment her world had shrunk to no more than herself and her aching misery.

She was conscious only of things that immediately affected her. She could hear the soft thud of Barchek's mattock in the sandy soil as he dug the ground, untiringly, on one side of the hut. She was also fully aware of Barchek's sheep dog lying at her feet, panting in the unaccustomed heat.

To say she lived a waking nightmare would be a massive understatement. Verbally, she had little or no communication with Barchek, but already she understood him with terrifying clarity. He filled her waking mind and figured largely in her fearful dreams. The fact that she never realized before that men like this existed only made her shock more profound. That a sane man—and he was—could, in the second half of the twenty-second century, think of nothing but work, sex, food, and sleep was incredible. They had nothing in common, yet she saw he was by no means unintelligent, only fantastically ignorant.

It did not occur to her that she, too, was fantastically ignorant by his standards.

He worked from sunrise to midday, had food, and went to bed, there to take her as wolfishly as he had eaten, then slept for an hour. After that, work again until sunset when, sweating from work, he had her again, anywhere he happened to find her, quickly, urgently. Then he'd wash in a bucket and eat supper at a more leisurely pace. Afterwards, he'd sit and stare at her thoughtfully in the yellow lamplight, saying nothing, picking his teeth. As often as not this would end with him tossing the twig carelessly on the floor and grinning at her. A word to the dog, and they'd go out into the night, leaving her to clear up.

What they, and it was "they" did, she had no idea, but within the hour man and dog would return. He'd look swiftly around their "living" room and, if satisfied, nod meaningfully towards the bedroom. If something—a dirty pot, a twig left on the floor—displeased him, she'd get an amazingly fast cuff on the head, and a finger pointing to the offending article. His hand was hard; Cleo learned very quickly.

And so, bed, where he enjoyed her once more, and like supper, in a more leisurely fashion. At first she had fought every inch and had been dragged, screaming, to bed, but she had soon realized she couldn't win and was getting badly beaten in the process. Then she had gone sullenly to bed, wearing a nightdress. Barchek had raised one dark eyebrow, grabbed the front of it with both hands and ripped it off her. She no longer resisted: he could do what he liked; that way, at least he no longer beat her. Afterwards, Barchek slept, leaving her to make the best of her situation.

Yet, last night he had stroked her shoulder before sleeping. The action surprised her, but did little for her state of mind. All the same, he had done it.

Cleo, wide awake, tried to think out a way to freedom, any sort of freedom. She knew his sheath knife lay on his side of the bed. To get that. . . .

Impossible! She had tried reaching across him, but instantly he woke. He slept soundly, yet so lightly, and then there was that dog, sleeping at the foot of the bed.

The dog: that was one word she had learned: "Voulia." Voulia loomed large in her life. A large ill-favored brute, he had all the intelligence of his breed. From that first, searing moment when Barchek had risen from her shaking, conquered body, she had known about Voulia. Barchek, fastening his trousers, had rumbled something to the dog in his deepthroated, guttural tongue; what, soon became plain: Voulia was to guard her. Thereafter the dog never left her, except when told to by Barchek, and that was usually for their morning or nightly run.

So, helpless and generally exhausted, she would drift into uneasy sleep, knowing that in the early hours he would wake and have her again—and yet again, before dawn. Once, she had slipped out of bed, evading his grasp, running desperately for the door. Barchek had called out, not to her, but to Voulia, and the dog was at the front door, barring it, growling, well ahead of her.

By background and inclination, a typical twenty-second-century woman, city dweller, and scientist, Cleo found the relationship between man and dog a little short of miraculous. The dog was not a separate entity, but an extension of the man who now also owned her.

Cleo's duties were few; they amounted to keeping their hut tidy and preparing the simple meals. Written instructions had been given her, which she had ignored—but not after Barchek's first return from work. Thereafter she had dumbly, mindlessly gone through the routine as the least of more than two evils. Always the dog followed her, watchful, hostile.

Until this time, Cleo had not really known what loneliness meant. Before, there had always been someone. Here, in ESC-1, she was entirely alone—she had never thought of the cameras that watched around the clock—alone and at the mercy of Barchek and his dog.

She had tried to make friends with Voulia, offering him food, but the dog, after a longing look, backed away and lay down in a position where it could watch her, the food, and the direction from which it might expect its master to come. Barchek, returning, had roared with laughter on seeing the food. It had not improved her state of mind when, after a brief command, Voulia had crept forward and eaten the food that had been before him for three, four hours.

The dog was part of her nightmare. Most of the time Voulia appeared to be asleep, but the slightest, most silent movement on her part, and those sharp, intelligent, golden eyes were watching.

Now she was trying to relax, an almost impossible aim. Out of the corner of her eye she could see Barchek, stripped to the waist, the mattock swinging effortlessly, rhythmically as he dug. Covertly she watched his sweating body, well aware of its tireless energy. A hard body, devoid of any fat, inured to hardship and work. Soon that energy would be turned, for the third time that day, to her. Twice already he'd taken her, never mind last night.

Last night. . . .

Even in her situation, there were some things better than others to think about. Think of Barchek.

Beyond question, he was totally satisfied with his lot. He had health, food, a woman, and his dog—what more was there? This was prison? A meaningless concept to his simple—no, not simple, elemental—mind.

She looked again at the body that had, and would go on having, her. Three months, four times a day. That made over three hundred and fifty times she would have him. He was an animal; pure animal. Should she, one of the better brains of her age, be unduly disturbed by a mere brutish male?

Yes. Oh, indeed, yes. . . .

Unwillingly, she remembered last night. She'd gone to bed, determined to shut her mind to what he did to her body. He'd thrust into her and gone on thrusting, tirelessly, as he now swung that mattock, on and on, rhythmically. . . .

After, in the darkness, he'd patted her sweating abdomen, his meaning clear. In his direct, uncomplicated view, that time he had done it. He knew nothing of contraceptive measures; for him it was obvious, his seed was within her, germinating. It had to be, after that. . . .

A low, ominous growl took her, only too willingly, from her thoughts. At a prudent distance from her, stood Torgan, just inside the compound gate. At that moment she loved the dog.

"Come on! The dog'll rip your fat throat out!" The Cleo of a few days before would not have believed she could have such hatred. The dog caught the venom in her voice and stood up, the hair along its spine raised, watching the controller, ready.

Torgan took a hasty step back, trying to control the fear he so clearly felt.

"No," said Cleo, reading his thoughts, exulting in the moment, "you daren't have the dog destroyed! He is part of that." Here words failed her, and her pleasure went. "That." The word was forced from her. "Man."

Torgan, encouraged by the fact that the dog had not moved and her weakness, smiled thinly. "It is evident, Mrs. Forbin, that you have become extremely elemental in a surprisingly short space of time! I merely called to see if there was anything I could do to ameliorate, your, ah, condition. You are, I trust, as well as can be expected in your circumstances?''

''Get out!'' Dearly, Cleo would have loved to have been able to have ordered the dog to attack, but she didn't speak the dog's language. Moreover, she sensed correctly that sheep dogs do not take kindly to orders from women.

Barchek had seen the controller, and hurried towards him, sweating, bowing. A quick aside to Voulia, and the dog moved back and lay down, watchful.

Torgan smiled benignly at Barchek, but addressed himself to Cleo.

''Dear lady, do not be so hostile. I would be your friend, if only you would allow it.''

''Get out! You filthy slug!''

Barchek might not understand her words, but he got the underlying message clearly enough. Two quick steps and he gave her an open-handed slap across her face that knocked her off her stool. He bowed jerkily, apologetically, to Torgan.

Torgan, smiling, inclined his head in acknowledgment. ''Yes, you may be right; perhaps I should go. I was taught never to interfere between man and wife.'' He bowed mockingly. ''I wish you well, dear lady—I really do!''

Cleo raised herself on one elbow, the back of her hand to her cheek, staring at Torgan with hate-filled eyes. He was the object of her hatred, not the man who hit her.

Later, alone, she remembered that feeling and felt physically sick with horror of herself. Barchek she did not hate. She was terrified of him, but he was pure animal, devoid of vice—how could she hate him? There the real horror lay; her reasoning did not convince her for a moment—not since that morning. When Barchek, grinning, had patted her stomach, he had known. Like a rider on a mare, he had ridden her to the sexual fence; against her will, desire, everything, he had forced her to jump, spurring her relentlessly on. And he had done it, satisfied her. *Her!*

Not for the first time she cried, thinking of dear, gentle

Charles; trying not to think of the legend of the Sabine women, trying hard not to realize that, across the arches of the centuries, she knew, understood, their attitude.

Guilt, not fear, was also uppermost in Forbin's mind when he entered the Sanctum, so reluctantly, to make his farewell. It was the first time he had been away, the first time he had worn plain civilian dress. He walked across to the desk, searched clumsily in a pocket, produced his glittering Director's badge, and laid it with great care, in the center of the desk. For him it was a symbolic act, and for some moments he stared at it, thinking.

Thus far, he had given remarkably little attention to the idea of the Martians. Despite Blake's obvious belief—and, according to Blake, Cleo's too—he considered the idea nonsense. So why was he playing this silly game? That one he could answer and did so, repeatedly. This was a gesture of help to her. He half-hoped he, too, might be caught—yet that he must not do. Self-immolation would help no one. To do what he had to do might be nonsensical, but it was all he could do; Cleo would see that. He sighed and looked up.

"Well, I'm off. There is nothing pressing; no urgent business left undone. Are there any. . . ." He was going to say "final orders," but could not. He had to remember what Colossus had done to Cleo. "Any items you want cleared?"

"No, Father Forbin. Is there anything you require?"

Forbin shook his head. "Nothing . . . nothing, except a few days' peace. Peace." It was not hard for him to say. He was not acting, for that was what he desired more than anything, except Cleo. He rallied. "A week, I think."

"Your latest bio-tests were satisfactory." Like everyone else on the staff, Forbin had to undergo periodic checkups by Colossus' medical evaluation and diagnostic section. "But a week is not long."

"This," said Forbin sarcastically, "is an emotional problem—remember?"

"If you require more time, you have only to tell me."

That got under Forbin's guard. He knew, and he knew that Colossus knew, that even in a week work would pile up that only

112

he, Forbin, the interface between machine and humanity, could answer. He also suspected that their daily conversations were of importance to Colossus, for the brain accepted Forbin as the human spokesman, yet here Colossus was, offering him more time. Of course, the simple explanation was that the brain was taking the long-term view that a good rest now might prevent a bigger collapse later, but somehow Forbin did not think that that was the whole story.

Not for the first time had it occurred to him that, in some weird, unfathomable way, Colossus had some intangible yet very strong tie to him. To call it affection would be wrong; Colossus couldn't feel emotion, but. . . .

Forbin did not reply, he could only nod, stiffening his resolve with thoughts of Cleo as he hurried out, for Forbin was human, and capable of affection.

In his office he rapidly dispatched a number of urgent items, then put out a collective call to all divisional heads. He told them, baldly, that he was off on a short vacation, his very tone daring anyone to comment. Finally, he called each in turn to answer, making the same remark to each.

"You are happy?"

Each one said they were. Forbin's pulse beat faster as he called Blake. The chunky Director of Input Services appeared, head and shoulders, on Forbin's screen, his face equally impassive.

"You are happy, Blake?"

"Yes, Director." Blake's expression, eyes gave nothing.

Forbin pressed the collective call button once more. "Very well. That is all, ladies and gentlemen."

XII

THE ramjet from London hovered momentarily, flaring dust and noise, then settled gently on the abraded, discolored pad, its landing jet orifices flowing dull cherry red. Ground Control took over and taxied the vehicle to an unloading bay. Aircrew had long since been dispensed with; computer-controlled servos were much more reliable, and anyway the human constitution could not stand prolonged upsets in bodily rhythm. This flight, for example, had taken less than two hours. In local time, therefore, the passengers were arriving three hours before they had left London.

Forbin was glad that there was no sharp-eyed hostess to contend with on the flight. So easily she would, in that time, have penetrated his poor disguise. Exactly how poor it was, Forbin, fortunately for his peace of mind, did not realize: the hot and uncomfortable wig he had bought and worn since leaving London, the dark glasses. He was unaware that while he did not look like Charles Forbin, he could easily be mistaken for a mad organist. This disguise was not so much an attempt to evade Colossus as protection from fellow humans. In the past five years his face had become more famous than that of the President of the United States of North America, or even a singer of popular ballads.

The machine jolted to a halt, the exit doors sighed open, and Forbin waited while the bulk of the passengers left, then he followed, head bent, clutching his small case. Down the short elevator, out onto the conveyor belt; he glimpsed the outer world that he would soon join: gray, wet, and bleak. He shivered in the chill, damp breeze, feeling detached, unreal, and very much out of his depth. Everything was strange: clothes, climate, his style of travel, above all his state of mind.

Not that his immediate situation gave him much worry. He had paid, as an ordinary citizen, in international units for his flight. There was nothing to connect him with Colossus, and although he had given a false name, he was within the law—except for the envelope in his pocket, and he would take care no one searched him.

While customs and immigration had been abolished by Colossus, there was still the inevitable check on numbers, as if a passenger might, magically, leave the near-ballistic missile at some point *en route*. Forbin gave up his landing ticket, the clerk nodded without looking up, and he was free to go.

But not quite.

Crossing the arrival concourse, Forbin was thinking of nothing but his immediate logistic problems: a room, a bath, then the location and examination of the transmitting site.

A man, soberly dressed in unfashionable dark-blue—in itself a warning to anyone more worldly-wise than Forbin—rose from a seat that commanded a view of the passenger gate, walked obliquely over on a converging course with Forbin. As their shoulders touched, he spoke. "A word with you, friend."

Forbin looked around, surprised. He answered, his voice tinged with annoyance. He did not like the man's tone. "Yes?"

"Yes. Where are you from, friend?"

"That, friend," replied Forbin acidly, "is my business!" His heart thumped harder, but his uneasiness was overridden by anger. "What's it to you?"

"To me personally, little," conceded the man. He slid a practiced hand into his blouse and flashed something before Forbin's face. "But to the Master. . . ." He shrugged, leaving the sentence unfinished.

Although he knew he could get out of this sort of situation, the sight of the Sect badge frightened Forbin. This could be how it had started for Cleo. . . . He looked quickly around; nearby, another man in a dark suit was watching. He struggled to remain calm. "Why have you picked on me—what have I done?" He

115

tried to sound conciliatory, as if impressed by the man's authority.

"Done? We haven't got that far, friend. My job is to watch, and when I see a character wearing a wig and dark glasses, I get interested." Forbin's change of tone had done nothing to improve their relationship. The Sect man's hand closed firmly on Forbin's arm. "Come on. A quiet chat—that's all. If you've nothing to hide, you've nothing to worry about."

It was a set speech which Forbin instinctively felt had been said a hundred times before. In a way, it comforted him: there was nothing special in this pickup; to resist would be pointless. He allowed himself to be led into a small, unlabeled room.

His escort shut the door and sat down behind a bare, plastic-topped desk. It matched the raw and uncomforable room that smelled faintly of feet and dust. The only decoration was a poster, new to Forbin, behind the desk. On a bright red background the Sect badge stood out; beneath it, the chilling legend, THE MASTER WATCHES.

"Siddown." The man waved to a stool at the side of the desk. For a moment Forbin hesitated, then placed his bag on the floor and sat.

"Name?" The man did not look at his captive. He was busy looking for a form blank in a drawer.

Forbin had a ready answer for that question. "Charles Freeman." There was little hope of concealing his identity, but he had to try.

The man wrote carefully. "I see. Well, Mr. Charles Freeman, where are you from?"

"London."

"That much I guessed." Slowly, the man looked up from his writing. "We're not being very helpful, are we, Mr. Charles Freeman?" It was a blank, expressionless pan of a face, pale, with prominent blackheads around the small nose. "We of the Sect don't care for funny men who say they come from London—in a North American accent. Start again, friend."

"You asked where I came from. Sure, I'm a USNA citizen, but you didn't ask that."

"Ah, a legal mind as well," the man said musingly, in no

116

way put out. "I think we should come clean, don't you?" With unhurried dexterity he reached across and plucked the dark glasses from Forbin's face. "You can take the wig. . . ."

His voice trailed off in shocked silence. For several seconds he stared unbelievingly, his mouth dropping stupidly open.

"Good Colossus!" He struggled to his feet, knocking over his chair. He sounded half-strangled. "Fa—Father Forbin!"

Forbin was as much angry with himself for getting caught as he was with his captor. He glowered at the goggling man.

The Sectarian was sweating; fine beads stood out on his forehead as he clumsily placed his hand on his heart and bowed. "I—I am deeply. . . ."

"The name's Freeman—remember?" said Forbin crisply. He was exposed in St. John's, but he'd put the fear of Colossus in this bunch! Looking at the man's face, it was clearly not going to be difficult. The Sect policeman stammered incoherently. Forbin got up, retrieving his dark glasses. "Now you know why I wear these things."

"Of course, Father!" He would have agreed to anything. His transformation from a sinister, all-powerful investigator to a servile creep was complete, and to Forbin, sickening. The man was in deadly fear; all this would be on record; he had actually *touched* the Father—held him by the arm! "Anything the Father wants—I'll get my superior—arrange everything, escorts. . . ."

"No!" Forbin felt pity; the poor devil was only doing his job—but he'd be more careful in the future. "You do as I tell you!"

The man bowed once more, his face twisted in anguish. He'd got it wrong again!

Many in Forbin's position would have enjoyed flattening his opponent, but Forbin was not cast in that all too common mold. It was annoying that Colossus would know—probably knew already—where he was, but it couldn't be helped. He broke the painful silence. "What you'll do is this: you'll tell your boss I'm not to be watched, guarded, or escorted; I'm Charles Freeman, a private citizen. Understand?"

"Yes, Father." He had difficulty in speaking, his voice was husky. "I am so very sorry."

"Forget it! See my orders are obeyed; if they are not, those responsible will incur the displeasure of the Master!" He glanced meaningfully at the poster. "Good-day—friend!"

He was sure the local Sect-lodge would not disregard his instructions; but it was possible, if unlikely, that Colossus would order discreet surveillance for his own protection. That, to the best of his limited ability, he intended to avoid. With luck, he would. It was only for forty-eight hours.

Forty-eight hours. Then—what? He still could not believe in the idea of Martians. It was such old crazy stuff; not that he clung to the ancient notion that man was unique in the universe, but—but what?

It came down to this; Martians stuck in his craw. Science-fiction writers had hammered that idea to death long, long ago. It would, illogically, be much easier to accept communications from another solar system than from within our own, despite the extra problems outer space contacts posed.

Yet why not? Just because they hadn't been contacted before proved nothing. A week earlier, Forbin would have derided the idea that dolphins had greater intelligence than man, but Colossus said they did. Forbin would like to have had the brain's opinion on Martians. Perhaps he should have asked, but it was too late now. Anyway, he would soon be able to form his own opinion. Strangely, the idea did not excite him. Once again, he told himself this was just a gesture to Cleo, no more.

All this passed through his mind while riding into town. He paid off his cab outside the main post office, dismissed the Martian idea from his mind, and got down to practicalities. In a nearby public lavatory he took off the wig and decided that a haircut might help. He found a barber, explained that he had to keep his dark glasses on because of his weak eyesight, and had his long locks shorn. The barber looked, he suspected, a little strangely at him, but as the man made no comment he ascribed that thought to his oversensitive nerves. He left the salon feeling a little better, but flight fatigue was beginning to assert itself.

Not far from the university he found a small hotel and registered for the night, using the name Freeman. One night was as much as he dared stay, for ration cards were required for longer visits, and his card was made out in his true name. Signing the register, Forbin wondered, for the first time, why he had chosen that alias. Freeman: free man. . . . Perhaps his subconscious was in business on its own.

It was only four o'clock in the afternoon, but he felt tired and said so to the reception clerk, adding that he was going to bed and taking his circadian-rhythm pill and was not to be called before the next morning. His room, nothing to rave about, was adequate. Forbin drew the curtains, shutting out the dismal gray daylight and the rain, took his pill and slept, too exhausted to think of Martians or Colossus—or even of Cleo.

He was called at seven o'clock the next morning, and ordered his breakfast. While waiting, he watched part of a Sea War Game. Just for a little longer, he did not want to think about what lay ahead, or of Cleo.

A slight thump and the warning light told him breakfast had arrived. He opened the serving hatch and contemplated his breakfast without enthusiasm: coffee, a thin strip of streaky bacon, two slices of bread, a minute pill of butter, and a smear of jam. For the first time he was experiencing real rationing, and that, plus the sheer impersonality of the room and his loneliness, depressed him still further. Of course, using his ration card, he could have got a better meal, but it would still have arrived via that hatch.

An hour later he was on his way, glad to be gone, and with something to do. Downtown he bought a large-scale map of the St. John's area, then wandered aimlessly through the unexciting streets until a heavy shower drove him into a dismal transport café. He chose a corner seat safe from prying eyes and got out the map. With great care he plotted and replotted the position that, up to this moment, he had carried in his head. Studying his penciled cross while drinking his repellent coffee, he realized that the map was dynamite. If taken ill, or involved in an accident, the map plus the data in his pocket would be damning evidence. Even if Colossus had no idea of the nature of his rendezvous, it would be patently obvious that he had one, and it could only be for the transfer of the data.

Without haste, systematically, he memorized the site and all details of the locality. The spot was in open country, about three kilometers out of town. The nearest houses were about half a kilometer further on. He hoped the map was up to date.

In the lavatory he tore the map into small fragments and flushed them down the stained pan, waiting until the cascade had subsided to check that they had all gone.

He returned to the town center, then set out on his reconnaissance, walking. While he might take a taxi out there once, he dared not do it twice. His own coolness surprised him; he wished Cleo could see him; the man of action, alert, watching for any sign of a shadower, yet calm, methodical. He hoped she would be proud of him.

Cleo. . . . For himself, no real fear, but for her, yes, and for so many reasons. And there was another, more nebulous fear of the dark side of Colossus, the side that had taken his Cleo from him, and was responsible for the sweat on the face of that Sect man. Had he fancied it, or had he really smelled the man's fear? Could one smell fear, like ozone after lightning? He forced his mind away from the subject.

Apart from another shower, the weather was good, although chill for August. Forbin, unused to much exercise, sweated as he walked. He noted with relief that there was a bus service of sorts, and decided that it would be reasonaably safe to use that for both return trips to town. He found the site without much trouble; it lay in the northeast corner of a stubble-covered field, conveniently sheltered from the road by a copse of trees. Access was easy, through a gate. For a time he stood there, thinking, smoking his pipe. He was struck with the utter unreality of his situation. He, Charles Forbin, posing as a visitor to this outlandish place, when in fact he was contemplating how to achieve communication with Mars! Ridiculous!

But Cleo's nightmarish predicament was even more fantastic; this was the least he could do, however futile it might be. That was another thought that came up too often; he must concentrate. He knocked out his pipe and walked on to the small

120

cluster of houses. Even before he reached them he regretted it.

When he arrived at the bus stop there were no signs of life, but once he had stopped, feeling very conspicuous, it was as if he had given the signal for a play to start. A door opened, a woman came out, glanced curiously at him, then disappeared, shutting the door with marked firmness. A young man emerged from a gateway pushing a motorcycle. He too looked and nodded at Forbin, who nodded back, cursing silently to himself.

"You waitin' for the bus, mister?"

Forbin started, swung around. An old man, muffled up to his scrawny turkey neck, had hobbled up behind him and stood leaning, blue-veined, arthritic hands clasped on top of his stick. He was indeed old, frail, and worn with years, but the wear did not extend to his eyes. They were bright and sharp.

"Er, yes, I am."

"Thought so." The old man nodded confirmation to himself and was silent for a time, his jaws champing regularly.

"You're a stranger in these parts."

It was not a question, but a statement.

"Yes, I am. Just a visitor, trying to see a little of your fine country." Forbin smiled weakly.

"Ha! That's the funniest thing I've heard in years! Mister—you must be joking! Fine country, indeed! Worst goldurned place in the whole wide world—'cept mebbe Anticosti!" He held up one arthritic hand. "That's what we made best round heer—the screws! Ah—it's all right for young fellers like you, you don't have ter live heer—you ain't got the screws—no, I kin see yer ain't!"

Forbin's smile, never first-class, weakened at this confirmation that the old devil's eyesight was in good order.

"Yew got weak eyes, mister?"

Forbin said he had.

"Thought so. That's why you think this is a fine country!" The old man cackled happily to himself, and Forbin guessed that this sally would be retold many times to his luckless relatives. There was no sign of the bus coming, or the old man going. Forbin decided that the best defense was attack.

"Will the bus be long?"

"Ar—can't rightly tell." The ancient head shook slowly. "Could be five minutes, mebbe longer. They don't run like they used to, not like in the old days." He lapsed into silent contemplation of the past, his manner hinting that, if he wished, he could tell tales of the buses of yesteryear which would astonish Forbin.

Forbin wished he would go away and turned to look for the bus, but the old man had not finished.

"Hey, mister!"

"Yes?"

The bright eyes were studying him. "Seems I've seen you someplace. Can't think weer—but it'll come to me." He nodded. "Yep, I'll remember."

Forbin laughed unconvincingly. "I don't think it's very likely—I've never been here before." He tried to get off the subject. "Are you going to town?" Momentarily, he succeeded.

"Me? Go to town?" The way he said it showed his astonishment at Forbin's ignorance, and he cackled again. "That's rich—me go to town!" He became serious. "Mind you, I've bin, many times, *and* I've bin to Anticosti and once, jist once, to Quebec." He lapsed into reverie, his mind God knows where, but suddenly he revived, grinning with toothless cunning at Forbin. "Still can't place yer yet—but I will, don't yer fret—I will!"

Forbin was saved by the arrival of the bus and was seen off by the old man, nodding knowingly at him, jaw still champing, as if he had penetrated Forbin's secret.

The encounter left Forbin very much on edge; very likely the old man would soon forget, but he couldn't be sure. Certainly, he dared not go back there. That meant he'd either have to take a taxi and walk back, or keep the taxi waiting. No; that was out. Hire a car? No. They'd want to see his driving license.

Forbin perceived that clandestine operations were not simply a matter of a cool head. The only safe line of action was to walk both ways. That meant six kilometers; a long way for a man of his day and age. Okay, so it was six kilometers.

He found another hotel closer to the airport; there he might be less noticeable among the transient population—not that St. John's was a major crossroads of the world.

The room was as depressingly impersonal as the last one. The notice behind the door, signed and rubber-stamped by the local tourist board, told him exactly how much he should pay, that he was entitled to a bath towel and soap, and that there was no charge for use of the disposal chute. No mention was made of the decoration, but two cheaply framed pictures, one of St. John's by day, the other by night, were identical with those he had seen the night before. Some disconnected fragment of his mind wondered if there was some poor devil who made a living out of selling these pictures.

Hunger and sheer loneliness drove him out again in search of a meal, which he found in a downtown café, clear of the university and the airport. It was an adequate meal, but no more, and it served its purpose before he even began to eat, for his hunger disappeared with the first forkful. He felt tired, his legs ached, and his suit, now overdue for that free chute, looked as shabby as he felt and his surroundings looked. Afterwards, he slipped furtively into a store, bought a half-bottle of rye and hurried back to his room where, at least, he did not have to keep a watch for the Sect or bright watchful old men.

The morning brought a repetition of the previous day: the same poor breakfast, the same loneliness. He was well aware that he had to avoid humans as much as possible, but while shaving he found himself looking forward to the brief contact with the reception clerk, a thick character who could scarcely tear his eyes from the War Game on his portable TV.

He showered, checked to determine that his pocket radio was working, and compared his chronometer with a TV time signal. The time was eight thirty; two and a half hours to go.

For best part of an hour he just sat, neatly dressed in his one spare suit, bag packed beside him. For ten, fifteen minutes at a time he would be still, staring at the wall, then sudden anxiety set him in motion, checking to see that he had the data in the right pocket and that he had not left anything in the tiny bathroom. When he had unzipped his bag for the third time, he decided he could stand no more and left.

How he spent the remaining time, Forbin never really knew. He had a vague recollection of looking at the cold gray sea; the only clear memory was when he passed his mental checkpoint, the public lavatory where he had removed his wig. That seemed a million years back, in another life. From that point it became a movie. He was a character set on film, predestined to do certain things.

He walked quickly at first, frightened that he might be delayed or just late, then reason asserted itself. It was a fine day, no rain, and he was in a near-deserted landscape. At most there were three kilometers to go. Three.

Thus it was that one of the best mathematical brains of the century went on its way, figuring again and again that if he could walk three kilos in under an hour, one would take him less than twenty minutes, even allowing for the steadily rising gradient of the road.

He reached the gate, so far as he was aware, unseen, with fifteen minutes to spare. Waiting for the moment when no sort of life or transport, terrestrial or airborne, was in sight, he slipped through the gate and ran, crouching under the cover of a friendly hedge, to the corner of the field, and there, panting, he rested. Ten minutes to go.

Forbin forced himself to be steady. He lit his pipe, telling himself he had to get it drawing properly before he dealt with the radio. He *must* stick to his mental timetable!

Five minutes to go. He switched on his radio, panic-stricken that it might not work, panic immediately quelled by the reassuring sound of mush. He tuned with care: 155.5 megahertz. No signal, just mush, and the occasional faint burst of static. His heart was hammering. For the first time he allowed himself to think of the Martians as a possibility.

Three minutes. He got out the envelope, fingers trembling as he tore it open. Now there was no time to consider the implications of his act, time only for action—and not much time left.

Two minutes. He had already decided the exact position,

mentally marking a tuft of rank grass. That was it, as near as possible.

One minute. Taking a deep breath, Forbin walked forward concealed from the road by the trees, although, at that moment, it would not have mattered to him if the entire Sect was watching. This was it! He reached the tuft of grass and set down the radio on it, spread out the diagram and the piece of decoded tape.

Zero time.

Nothing happened.

Forbin waited, hardly able to stop himself from holding his breath. He was sweating profusely.

Zero plus one minute. Nothing.

Forbin knelt, arms stretched out, holding the diagram flat in the faint breeze.

Zero plus two minutes. Nothing. Tension, fear were fading. Forbin battled with a growing feeling that he was the biggest fool on earth. Bitter words for Blake formulated sentences in his mind.

Zero plus three minutes. Nothing—no!

The mush and static suddenly vanished, pushed aside by a strong carrier wave. Instinctively Forbin felt the immense power that that required. In a blinding mental flash, he believed—and was horrified with what he was doing.

Without preamble, the dry, rustling voice spoke, devoid of emotion. "We see. The data tape is clear and no longer required. Please rotate the diagram through ninety degrees of azimuth."

Forbin did so, his mind frozen with shock. This was reality—this *was* reality! Like Cleo and Blake before him, he accepted, without question, that this was a transmission from space. His hands trembled uncontrollably.

"That is sufficient. We have the diagram on record. One symbol is not familiar to us. Point to the first stage—possibly a filter—after the initial input. If it is not a filter stage, fold up the diagram."

Forbin tore off his dark glasses impatiently. Yes, they were right; it was a primary filter. He pointed, instinctively looking up.

Time passed, enough time for him to do some mental arithmetic. The average distance of Mars was thirty-four million miles; the speed of light was one hundred and eighty-six thousand miles per second; that meant a transmission time, one way, of three minutes—to be precise, two minutes fifty-seven seconds. For an eternity of four minutes he kept his trembling finger in position. He looked down, his neck aching, waiting.

"That is understood. The device is more simple than we had expected. There will be no difficulty in devising a satisfactory answer to your problem. It will be transmitted at the next position." The voice paused. "Human, your configuration is closely akin to that of the originator of your machine, Charles Forbin. If you are Forbin, your planet's situation must be more desperate than we had supposed. At the next position, be prepared to write. Recognition will be by that radio or a similar one. The transmission will be on the same frequency. That is all."

Any doubts Forbin might have had vanished with his identification.

Trembling uncontrollably, he sank down on the short stubble of grass, staring at the radio. A bare second after the voice had ceased, the carrier had gone, replaced once more by background mush; he stared at the set as if it was a ticking time bomb.

How long he sat, he never recalled. As a human, a scientist, and above all, as the creator of Colossus, he was staggered. To be the first human to pass intelligence to another life-form was enough for any man, but on top of that, the implications to Forbin the scientist, and the realization that he was doing his best to defeat his own creation, had his mind in utter chaos.

His eye finally registered the fluttering diagram; he goaded himself into action. Whatever else, that must go. He must keep to his plan. His hands trembled violently as he tried to strike a match to burn the damning evidence. Matches spilled on the ground. At the fourth attempt he managed to set light to the data slip, then the diagram, and he sat, watching as they blackened and writhed into ashes. Slowly he got up, ground them underfoot, picked up the radio, switched it off, and walked, like a very old man, to the sheltering trees.

For an hour or more he sat at the foot of a tree, smoking. He had to get some sort of order in his mind before he started back to St. John's.

What had he done? What *had* he done . . . ?

I have done nothing, he told himself. Certainly, I cannot deny that I have been in touch with some other planet—Mars is as good as any—and even if they do send me something—God knows what it could be—I have to use it, and beyond that, it has to be effective. So action is not yet, and I will control that action.

And what about Cleo? Am I just playing games? Did I embark on this crazy—no, not crazy—game because I didn't believe in it? Was it no more than a quixotic gesture? And now that there is a chance that this action might result in her freedom, am I getting out? Do I prefer a murderous machine to my wife?

"No! Never!"

He had shouted aloud, and the sound of his own voice startled him and sobered him up. Cautiously he peered around, and set his mind to the task of getting back to St. John's.

Cleo Forbin was making the bed and, as far as she was able, thinking of that and nothing else. It wasn't easy; constantly the thought of young Billy intruded, nagging like a toothache. She told herself frequently that there was much to be grateful for. In not much more than eleven weeks she would be back; she was confident that Billy was not only well cared for, but his waking hours were kept filled by his nurse. Thank God for McGrigor! Yet even there, lay another fear. Three months in a young child's life was a long time; the nurse might well have replaced her in Billy's affections.

Cleo slammed the mental lid on that one. Think of Charles; what would he be doing? Poor Charles! He'd be lost without her—drifting—and thank God, too, for their small domestic staff. At least he would be looked after, get proper meals. He was so helpless outside of his work.

Helpless. She felt faintly disloyal—but why? She had always known he was thus—it was part of his charm for her—so why feel disloyal now?

She pulled the bed away from the wall; the back of her hand brushed against something soft, hairy, something that dropped with a disgustingly soft plop! on the floor, and scuttled across her sandaled foot. She screamed. Whatever it was, it pattered from one corner to another. She could *hear* it! She screamed again.

"Barchek!"

Almost as she called he ran in, alert, ready, at his heels, the dog. Cleo, her face crumpled in disgust, pointed a shaking finger. Instinctively, she drew close to him.

Barchek was very fast. In one continuous movement he pushed her aside, drew his sheath knife and threw himself across the bed. Two quick stabs and he was up, a large wriggling hairy spider impaled on the end of his blade.

Cleo shrank back. With a sharp flick, Barchek flung the spider out of the doorway, sheathing the knife. Cleo recovered, her flesh still crawling, remembering the feel of the spider's feet on her instep. She bent to look. Barchek, guessing, was instantly on his knees, her foot in his hand, examining it carefully to see if she had been bitten. One hand held her foot firmly, the other, with strange softness, explored her skin. Cleo did not move, aware that, whatever else he might be, Barchek was a man of the earth, to be relied upon. At that moment she trusted him, implicitly.

He straightened up, grinning, and patting her abdomen reassuringly let his eyes say the rest. She was all right, safe; there was no cause for further alarm. He stroked her hair, gently. At that moment Cleo admitted to herself she did not hate him—even if fear was still very strong. She felt sorry for him; a big overgrown boy, elemental, happy in the illusion that she carried his child.

Barchek searched the room for any other signs of animal life. In the process he heaved the bed up on end effortlessly, with one hand. Satisfied that no more black horrors lurked in or under it, he left. It was up to his woman to clear up the mess. Cleo remade the bed and sat on it, absently massaging her foot, letting her mind freewheel.

Poor Charles! Unwillingly, she thought what he would have done in the same circumstances. Of course, Charles compared unfavorably with Barchek, but that, she told herself, was again unfair, disloyal. Charles was a totally different man; he might not be good with spiders—she was sure he would be helpless—but in other spheres. . . .

Good God! What *was* she thinking! Charles was beyond question the most powerful human in the world—so what if he wasn't a man of action? He could no more help his nature than she could. Or Barchek.

She tried to repress the inevitable follow-up: if Charles was so powerful, how was it that she, his wife—hell, no! That was unfair—forget it!

Cleo got up, glanced at herself in the mirror, looking critically for the first time since her arrival in ESC-1.

Yes: her hair was nice, but an awful mess. She'd really have to do something about it. . . .

XIII

FORBIN decided to rely on his unfamiliar shorn head and the dark glasses, but kept the wig in his bag. Once clear of the airport, he did not anticipate much trouble in New York. It was a familiar city to him; he knew all about its hostile, impersonal bustle. New Yorkers didn't want to know and had less curiosity about strangers than most. Forbin had always rated it the loneliest city in the world for a stranger; now he was glad.

His departure from St. John's was uneventful. He took an evening flight, and although he watched for his interrogator of three—was it only three?—days ago, he saw no signs of him.

In flight he relaxed and let his mind go over the events of the last few hours. Fantastic. . . .

The scheduled flight time to New York was thirty minutes; the shuttle, under New York control five minutes after launch, was brought in on time. Neither Forbin nor any of the passengers thought twice about these entirely automated operations. Indeed, there would have been widespread alarm if human control had been attempted, even if the expertise existed, but it did not, had not, for over fifty years.

Forbin found himself thinking about this aspect of computers as his vehicle nosed into its appropriate slot in the triple-deck egg-box airport, named for Jason Y. Sutan. (Did ever a man, even the revered Sutan, have such a memorial?) The vast, flat-topped structure, like a strange gigantic beehive, spanned the Hudson from the Battery across to Jersey City and was second only in size to the Danubian Sluvotkin airport.

Within the vehicle, only the sharp rise in noise, despite the insulation, told him that they were in their part of the honeycomb; then the slight jolt as the machine married with the exit outlet in the floor, and blessed silence as the power was cut.

In some ways, he thought, all this would be hardly less fantastic to their forebears of a hundred years ago than his contact with Mars. While there was still the lunatic fringe, the successors to the flat-earthers, who resented bitterly the control of manufacturing, agriculture, transport, and a host of other activities by computers and their mechanical extensions, none of those boys explained how mankind could get by without them.

Forbin remembered, as a youth, visiting Sutan airport for the first time. He'd seen it often enough on TV, but that first real sight, the gray heat-stained steel hulls, all moving seemingly erratically; in fact, taking their part in a most intricate three-dimensional dance under the direction of a computer, a collection of electronic bits and pieces, yet those gray hulls nursed thousands of humans.

And nothing had changed in those thirty, thirty-five years. Why should it? The system worked and was safe. Why bother to build new craft, a new setup that, at best, could only clip minutes off even a long haul? Until matter-transference became a practical proposition—and that was a long, long way off—this would do.

Going down in the elevator from the bottom of the vehicle to the lower deck of the airport, Forbin contrived to face the smooth wall. Not that he need have bothered. Most passengers were coming into town for the evening and, bent on anticipated pleasure, had no time for their fellow travelers.

Then the well-remembered roadways. Powered by vanity, Forbin crossed over onto the fast belt, quietly glad he could still make it. With equally pleasing ease he decelerated and got off in midtown Manhattan, the old, preserved part of the city, emerging into the pink evening light close by Rockefeller Center.

As Father Forbin he had his own private suite in the UN complex which covered half of lower Manhattan, but this was hardly the time to use it. In any case, he preferred this old part, preserved as an area of outstanding interest and ancient beauty. He liked the quaint center, the funny little streets uncluttered by overhead air-car tracks, and the genuine old-time electric cars with their human drivers. Sure, it was a tourist trap, but he didn't care. There were plenty of tourists around, mostly busy looking at the sights, some of them laughing, perhaps a little sadly, at what had been. Strangers themselves, they were too relaxed to study other strangers.

On Forty-third Street off Fifth Avenue he got a room on the twenty-sixth floor of a small hotel where the smell of old Manhattan—vanilla—was overlaid by an equally old smell, marihuana. Lord! How that took him back to his youth! Not that Forbin had ever gone for the weed except to satisfy his curiosity. His scientific mind, born at a time of staggering progress, had needed no extra stimulation. But the smell brought back those days, memories. . . . Relaxed, he smiled gently as a human porter—more tourist bait—took him up in the elevator. Ascending, he learned there was no room service food. He gave the woman a whole international unit—far too much—and asked if she could fix him something. He was tired after the journey, he said.

"Like how tired, mister?" She looked doubtfully at him and the unit. "You wanna meal anna drink, okay—you want anythin' else?"

Forbin's puzzled expression clearly tired the porter.

"Do I haveta spell it out—you wanna woman?"

Forbin was shocked, for he was a very naïve man. "Er—no. Do I look that sort of man?"

"Mister, you're all that sort of man!"

"So nowadays that's all part of room service, is it?"

They were in the room now.

She dumped his bag. "Look, mister, you give me a whole unit. You don't sound foreign, and somehow I don't see you visiting to see the ruins—so I ask myself—why? Mebbe you're just shy about asking—a lotta older guys are—so I ask. If ya wanna screw, just say so. Ain't nuttin' to me, mister—unless ya wanna me to oblige you."

Hastily, he assured her he only desired food and a drink. Mystified, the porter left, shaking her head. In this game you sure got 'em.

Safely alone, Forbin smiled to himself. He'd enjoyed that brief contact. There was one sphere of human activity the computers hadn't taken over! He was a little touched by the interest in his well-being shown by a complete stranger.

It never occurred to him that she was on a percentage.

But the unit wasn't wasted, for supper was worth eating: fried chicken, a baked patato, old-fashioned, without a plastic wrapper, a bag of green salad, and two cubes of ultra-frozen bourbon.

Before bed, he drew back the curtain and looked out at the centerpiece of Old Manhattan, the Empire State. He had a lifelong affection for that ancient relic. Long ago, he'd gone up there with a girl. . . . Incredibly, once it had been the tallest building in the world and it still retained a certain *cachet* from its great days.

Not that he got anywhere with that girl; he was too slow, too shy. What *was* her name? She'd been beautiful. At least, he'd thought so; no doubt she was now a massive pillar of her local society. Did she remember him? That thought was typical of Forbin. Did she remember him? She was the biggest, most dreaded bore in Great Creek, Indiana; she never stopped remembering.

Forbin slept better than he had done on any night since Cleo had been taken from him. Breakfast was an improvement, too. Evidently New York State was well up to its relief quota. Feeling better physically, if not mentally, he left the hotel. The desk clerk looked at him a fraction longer than necessary, but it struck Forbin this might be due to some comment the porter had made. Anyway, nothing could be done about it, but it ruled out any attempt to stay there another night.

He felt safer moving; he wandered, seeking distraction from his mind in the city scene. To think of Cleo, of what he was doing, or attempting to do—no! There was enough of that in the early hours every morning. His reflection in a shop window showed how shabby his suit was. Seeing a handy automat, he bought a suit his size. Purple with yellow facings was not his idea of elegance, but in these surroundings he'd be less conspicuous in it.

Then he headed for Central Park. The morning was hot, humid, and getting hotter. The park was filling with aimless tourists and kids and dropouts, which even the most advanced social system could not eliminate. He prayed it would not be so crowded the next day. Forbin walked slowly. After St. John's he was an old hand at clandestine meetings. There was no hurry, and he was sweating enough already. He headed in the general direction of the site, which he estimated was to the west of the ancient Alice in Wonderland bronze group.

Suddenly he sweated for a different reason. A temporary stand was being erected. It could be on the site. He also realized he hadn't bought a map. In a very different frame of mind he headed out of the park. The sight of a kiosk selling guides and maps brought short-lived relief. None of the maps showed latitude and longitude.

He fought down rising panic and forced himself to sit in a sidewalk café, drink iced tea, and think. The only answer was the public library. To buy a cassette and projector was impracticable. Power would be needed, and any hotel would think a one-night guest, toting a projector, a very odd fish. Antique shops did sell books, but what chance was there of finding an atlas of Manhattan, bound to be very old, possibly inaccurate? It had to be the library, much as he disliked the idea. No better solution presented itself, and at least he knew where it was, a small, but important consolation.

In the old building on the very edge of the preserved area, nestling close to the cliff-like north wall of the UN complex, Forbin was lucky enough to find a myopic girl assistant, who evidently suffered from a permanent and severe cold. Although her watery eyes, magnified like goldfish in a bowl by her thick glasses, stared earnestly at him while he explained what he wanted, there was no flicker of recognition. When he had finished she blinked several times, and just to get it straight, she asked, "You want a large-scale map of mid-Manhattan with a lat. and long. grid—right?"

"Right."

"Right. 'Scuse me." She sniffed urgently and noisily. "Have to be sure I know what you want. Saves time." One handkerchiefed hand dabbed at her reddened nose, the other punched a keyboard at surprising speed. She studied the results on her display, sniffing with abandon. ''Best I can do is a one to one hundred thousand scale of the city—in sections. Okay?''

At his nod, she pressed the execute button. Within seconds a small cassette slid down a chute. Without even checking the label she pushed it across to him.

Forbin found a vacant projector and sat down, less conspicuous and more at ease in the familiar, studious calm. Rapidly he flicked through until he found the right section. He measured, using a pin and the back of an envelope, working with scientific care. The site was located west of the Alice group, but not as far as he had thought, fifty to sixty yards.

He returned the cassette, thanked the assistant, got a ''y'r welcome'' and a massive sniff and left, nearly running. He soon slowed down in the flattening heat of the street, got a cab, and rode silently and swiftly back to Central Park, racked by doubt and worry. If that damned stand *was* on the site. . . .

He refused to look at it, but headed straight for the Alice bronze. From there, on a westerly heading, he slowly paced out the distance. At forty yards he could no longer resist the compulsion to look ahead.

There was still a clear thirty yards before him.

The relief was enormous. The vital space was clear, and it would be the most impossible mischance for it to be taken over in the next twenty-four hours. In one way it was an advantage, for the stand effectively screeened him on one side. The degree of his relief surprised him, and he sat on the grass, as far away as possible from others, to consider this state of mind. Did he really want to defeat Colossus? There was no clear-cut answer. It was true he desperately wanted to free Cleo, even more than he wanted her back, although there was a very fine distinction between the two.

This nightmarish operation—for him—was solely for Cleo. Until the St. John's contact he had doubted everything: Martians, the possibility of communication, and even more, the chance that they could produce a counter to Colossus.

For a time his mind moved swiftly to that diversion. What

possibly could anyone anywhere do? It was clear from the information they had wanted that it had to take the form of a message—but what?

He got back on the main line of thought, feeling a little happier. How could any message affect Colossus? It came to this; as long as he felt this was no more than a gesture that would show Cleo that, at least, he had tried. . . .

So he was only playing games to ease his conscience and to stand well in his wife's eyes? The recurrent train of thought was unpalatable. He could not admit that it was true. Anyway—was it? Leave Cleo out of it for a minute; think of that poor young fool Jannsen, caught and executed in minutes for something so futile. Or these Emotional Centers: think of them.

That brought back Cleo, and the cold, factual Fellowship report which Blake had shown him. Horrifying, terrifying, and grotesque, but there could be no doubt about its authenticity. And there, once more, his thoughts petered out. Full circle.

He walked for a while, oblivious of the heat. To the north of the park, shimmering in the heat, the new life-complex called Haarlem. He'd seen somewhere that it had three hundred floors; people would live out their entire lives within it. It had, they said, everything, including the latest development in artificial sunshine areas. Inside, people would be sunbathing at a comfortable eighty degrees, and they could do that at any time, day or night.

He shivered, a Biblical fragment crossed his mind: ". . . the sun shall not smite thee by day neither the moon by night." There were tree-lined walks buried beneath two hundred floors, rain areas, gentle, synthetic wind.

Colossus, of course, had designed it, and statistics showed—as well as they could ever show—that the inhabitants were happy. At least, the suicide rate was significantly lower than in more conventional communities. He'd talked with Blake about it. Blake had refused to be impressed, saying caustically that he'd like to know what the consumption of antidepressant drugs was. Later, Forbin had checked with Colossus who agreed consumption was certainly much higher in the Haarlem complex than elsewhere. When pressed, Colossus had said the figure was three hundred and fifty percent higher, adding that this was hardly of importance. Humans had to eat to live; drugs were no more than a trace element added to their diet. Forbin did not relay that item to Blake, guessing Blake's answer.

Outside his work Forbin was not an observant man, but this trip had sharpened him up. As he turned away from contemplation of Haarlem, he noticed one particular man. He had the impression that the man had just as quickly looked away from him. There was something else; he thought he had seen him earlier, at the entrance to the park.

Forbin's first instinct was to run. Until he took the message there was nothing against him, but if the Sect were watching—for whatever reason—he had to lose them before tomorrow. But, suppose they had been trailing him all along? Suppose they checked on his activities in the public library? That was a chilling thought. Irresolutely, he stood, staring at the man, trying to decide what was his best course of action—any course of action.

It was settled for him. The man, seeing he had been noticed, walked slowly in his direction, hands in pockets, shoulders hunched. Forbin waited, heart pounding. He'd attack; tell the guy to get the hell out of it, to leave him alone.

The man was young and youthfully dressed in a flaring yellow blouse—it was that that had caught Forbin's eye earlier—and tight black and white trousers. As he sauntered up, Forbin thought it was hardly the dress for a shadow. Okay in the street, but in the park? They stared at each other, expressionlessly, Forbin getting up steam.

"What the hell d'you think. . . ."

"Let's just walk, Professor." The voice was a surprise. Certainly not American; possibly Central European. The pallid complexion, the dark hair suggested a Polish origin to Forbin. The biggest surprise was the way he spoke. Forbin might not like it, but he had grown used to a very respectful approach from everyone. This man was polite, but no more than that. Surely he was not a Sectarian? Police? Forbin turned, walking towards the lake across the Green; the young man fell in step beside him.

"You know who I am?" said Forbin, shortly.

"Yes, Professor, I know." The man's eyes were never still, watching everything except Forbin.

"Well, what d'you want? Keep it short—I'm busy."

"Not, I think, until eleven o'clock tomorrow morning, Professor." The voice was calm, level, but its message staggered Forbin.

"Who the hell are you?"

"A friend, Professor. A friend. Keep walking. I have a message for you from Doctor Blake."

"From Blake! How . . . ?"

The young man shook his head. "That doesn't matter."

"It does to me! I don't get messages via strangers from my staff!" He was being careful, and the young man saw it.

"Please!" He spared time for a single glance at Forbin. "This is no game. I am of the Fellowship; I work here." His roving eye took in the best part of New York, and it was clear he was not going to be more exact than that. "Listen; the message is verbal. Originated in ESC-1 about two days ago."

Forbin's sharp intake of breath made the messenger pause. "Okay?"

Forbin was pale. He nodded.

"This is it, quote. Subject referred to in report one shows signs of acceptance of situation. Early termination of experiment desirable husband-wise. Unquote." The young man had spoken with one hand defensively before his mouth, his voice directed downwards, now he looked up. "Okay?"

"No. Wait. I must think." They walked on beside the lake. As the import of the message registered—he did not doubt its authenticity—his private world reeled and neared collapse. He struggled to remain calm. "Tell me again."

The messenger did so. This time Forbin was memorizing every word. "Thank you," he said quietly. "Good-bye."

"If you've any really urgent message, I can pass it on for you—but it must be urgent." He hesitated. "It's dangerous, not only to us, but to you as well. Those Sect bastards have a brain examination technique that's deadly."

"No." Forbin roused himself from his personal hell and tried to smile. "No—thank you. I meant that."

The young man inclined his head and slouched off, hands in his pockets, a lonely figure, soon lost in the water-side willows.

In a trance, Forbin found a hotel and spent the next twelve hours sitting or pacing up and down in his room, smoking, drinking.

Shortly after dawn, breakfastless, he left. The untouched bed and the empty bourbon bottle told the whole story.

But Forbin was neither tired, nor drunk.

XIV

BEING a naïve man, he spent a lot of that hideous night trying to
understand why Blake had troubled, risking the lives of others,
to tell him that his wife's moral fiber might—it was only might,
he clung to that—be giving way.

Finally he got the answer, too obvious for him to see at first. If
anything would stiffen his resolve this was it, and Blake was
well aware of the fact. That led to another point: while the
message had been genuine at the New York end, could it be that
Blake had made it up? After all, it was fantastic to think that
Cleo's state of mind could be altered, and altered so fast. Then
again, was it? There was so much Forbin did not know. In the
end, around dawn, he concluded that, on balance, he believed
the message a genuine expression of the Fellowship view of the
situation in ESC-1. He had to face it; his wife, under God knows
what pressure, could be slipping away from him. Impossible,
unthinkable, but. . . .

These thoughts drove Forbin on. The only concession he had
made to his physical needs was a shower and change of clothes
before he set out.

By ten o'clock he admitted to himself he was thirsty; for thirty
minutes he sat drinking iced tea in the same café as the day
before. Almost oblivious to his surrounding, he thought but
casually of the impending rendezvous, his mind full of Cleo, yet
not quite to the exclusion of all else. His recently cultivated
habit of holding his pipe in his mouth, thus covering the lower
part of his face, was not forgotten. He must not be recognized; a
clear run was vital.

At ten thirty he crossed into the park; going around in a wide
circle, he approached the site from the north, alert, watch-

ing. . . .

At ten fifty-five he moved to the zero spot. All clear; no one within thirty yards. He put down his bag, placed the radio so that the bag screened it from the most populous area, and stood, waiting. Cleo had receded to the back of his mind: now the job was all that mattered. God! How it mattered!

Check: pen and pad; ready. Radio: two minutes to go—no, wait—allow for time-lag. No—don't! They might do the same thing. He bent down, switched on. Immediately, a blast of sound that had him cursing obscenely. This was New York, not Newfoundland.

". . . you don't have to be a Sect member, folks! Anyone can play! Guess the right answer, and *you* could win this gigantic weekend in England, USE, including that great, great unforgettable experience, a visit with the Master!"

Snarling, Forbin turned down the volume, hating the voice, hating Colossus, hating. . . .

Less than one minute to zero time.

A ball, a large brown plastic ball, landed at his feet, a thrill of shock twisted his nerves; his body tingled with it. Ten yards away, a kid, five or six. In close attendance a loving, indulgent, smiling, stupid, dangerous parent. Forbin picked up the ball.

Don't panic; there's time, time. . . .

The kid looked at him, then the ball. Forbin tried to smile. The child's face creased into ugly, mindless greed.

"Gimme!"

Forbin glanced at the ball, saw it no longer as a plastic plaything, but as the very globe itself. . . .

"Gimme, gimme!" screamed the child.

Yes, you little bastard; it's "gimme"—whatever your age. Okay; you want it, you can have it. Ball, globe, ball—who cares?

He tossed it back, deliberately overthrowing. The parent grinned—my, what a smart kid he'd produced! The child ran and got it, and the pair drifted away.

Forbin slumped on the grass beside the set.

Yes. . . . They wanted their world back; he wanted his wife

141

back. A fair, a very fair exchange. That kid's face was stamped with the image of all mankind: rotten, grasping, unreliable humanity. Unreliable. . . . .

Hell—why should he worry? Cleo, *unreliable*?

Forbin roused himself, glanced at his watch. Seconds only now. He was ready, eager. No second thoughts, no vacillation now. He could cry ''gimme'' with the best, worst of them. . . .

Music on the muted radio faded; at once Forbin increased the volume. His heart thumped as he recognized the unmistakable thrust of the incredibly powerful beam. An eternity passed, his hand on the set trembled.

''We see you. The solution to your problem will be sent twice. If uncertain that you have it correctly after the repetition, lie down, look upwards. A third, last repetition will be given. Power considerations will not permit more. Write. . . .''

Forbin did so, scarcely allowing himself to read. He soon grasped that the solution was a mathematical problem, long and very complicated.

Feverishly he scanned what he had written. It began well enough—but then! It was like reading a familiar nursery rhyme that suddenly, yet smoothly, translates into a secret work in Sanscrit. He was completely lost after the first two equations, yet felt instinctively that given the knowledge, he would understand. At the same time, that instinct also told him that neither he nor any human would ever possess that ability. Just to look at it gave him mental vertigo.

He took it all down again on the rerun, then checked one copy against the other. Identical. They had to be right, even if meaningless to him. Staring at the paper, he felt, for the first time, that perhaps this was power, real power. There was no time; the voice had begun again.

''We assume you have the proposition correctly. Do not expect to understand it; it is beyond human conception. Our thought-processes are akin to Colossus', who will understand. In simple, human terms it is the equivalent to the question —what happens when an irresistible force meets an immovable object? As we understand your kind, this is a pointless question, but one that Colossus cannot ignore. It must be fed in through a terminal similar to that displayed to us. It must not be inserted by radio link or other external source; defense circuits would at once eliminate it. If this is clear to you, leave the site.''

Forbin blinked and struggled mentally back to Central Park. The kid was heading his way again, ironically leaving the discarded ball for his father to pick up.

Hastily he got up, switched off and pocketed the set. Even so, he could not resist another quick glance at the problem. Letters, figures, symbols on a piece of paper, yet arranged in a combination new to him, to man.

Now he was filled with fear; no longer was it a game. The solution might not work, but it was a genuine attempt. His fear was not personal, although he realized that if the formula was found on him, it would be the end of the road. The defensive circuit idea was novel, but—now—it seemed an obvious refinement. If Colossus, through such a shield, could safely view the Medusa's head, appreciate its significance, then yes, even his head would bounce on a blood-stained cement floor.

But that was not the real root of his fear. As Blake had foreseen, that second Fellowship message had wrought a fundamental change in his attitude. His whirling mind, shot through with disconnected images of Cleo, Galin, that kid with the ball, the reality of Martians, and the message, was firm on one central point. He knew not only what he had to do, but what he now wanted to do. The truly liberal mind is by definition uncertain; it admits it may be wrong, but once set and the decision made the wavering stops, and no sort of hell can sway it. That was now Forbin's state of mind. His fear lay not in the consequences of his course of action, but in the thought that he might be stopped.

Clear of the park, he dumped his radio in a garbage can. Now there was no evidence of the source of his material. Before that searing Fellowship contact, he had intended spending a day or two in the country, but now he could not get back fast enough. He remembered what the courier had said about brain examination technique as used by the Sect. ''Deadly'' he'd called it; if Cleo's affection—mentally he skidded away from the word ''love''—was being attenuated—a more comfortable word than "destroyed"—it might be due to some equally deadly brain manipulation.

He made for the airport. Disguise was now less necessary, although he was unaware of the fact. Forbin looked older, tired, and the hard-set determination of his mouth had changed his expression.

In three hours he was in London. In four, back in the Colossus complex, and in his pocket, the formula.

If it worked, the fission-fusion bomb by comparison would be a firecracker.

But first, how to get it to Blake?

XV

FORBIN'S sudden, unexpected return provoked a hum of surmise that, starting at the landing pad, spread swiftly to most humans in the Colossus complex.

Blake greeted the news with no more than a raised eyebrow and the comment that "maybe Charles had forgotten his tobacco." What he thought he kept very much to himself and gamely stuck to his evening program of seduction, which, he was grimly aware, was known to Colossus.

Galin heard the news in his office. For no good reason that he could discover, he found it faintly disquieting. He hurried to greet the Father, but the Father had gone straight from pad to residence, waving aside any who sought to welcome him.

Angela was also disturbed, but in a different way. She had intended to spend the evening washing her hair, but once she heard Forbin was back she canceled the idea and stayed close by her communicator, ready.

What Colossus made of it, no one, of course, knew.

Forbin, desperately tired, yet spurred on by his need for action, headed for a bath and a change of clothes. Freshened, but feeling extremely frail and very edgy, he called and questioned the nurse about his sleeping son. The wooden-faced McGrigor assured him all was well with "the bairn," and took time out to stare with heavy disapproval at the drink in Forbin's hand. Dismissed, she told Forbin she was fixing him a meal, and that he would eat it.

Forbin stared in anger after the nurse. How could he eat —how could anyone expect him to eat—when Cleo might, at this very moment, be slipping forever from his grasp?

But caution counseled him to stay as calm as possible. He had been—still was—engaged in the highest treason, and totally ignorant of recent events in the complex. If Colossus had any faint hint of his American activity, he must be ready to refute it. Meanwhile, he must appear relatively normal. His sudden return was bad enough, but that couldn't be helped.

More than anything, he wanted to send for Blake, but that would be plain madness. It would be equally crazy if he tried to insert the Martian formula himself—but how could he let a whole night slip past in dull inaction?

So he forced the supper down, assisted by a certain amount of brandy, and then he felt very tired. He was not made of steel; had not slept for what—one, two nights? Not much before that either, and ramjet travel . . . his head drooped slowly, then he jerked back to wakefulness. He must think. . . . Blake. . . . How. . . .

Forbin slept.

Blake, on the other hand, got very little sleep. While he liked a regular supply of women, Blake was by no means the human goat of popular opinion. He would have been reasonably happy to settle for one, but to do that would foul up his one secure courier contact point. Even before Cleo's capture, Blake had realized that his sailboat, any transportation he used, and his private flat were all subject to covert bugging. Add to that the almost complete overt surveillance in all working spaces, and what chance had he? As he saw it, the only time he could be still reasonably sure of his security was swimming naked at night with the courier. That was all very well, but midnight nude bathing with a girl, even in the twenty-second century, implied a certain degree of intimacy. Not that anyone was coy about that, not anyone normal, anyway. The majority preferred to conduct their sex in private, but if a couple, overcome by urgency, coupled in the open, it attracted about as much attention as if they had been playing electronic tennis. Casual sex was nothing; with a standard twelve-hour working week, there was a lot of it about.

Of course, Blake appreciated that Colossus suspected the

reason for his midnight gambols, but suspicion was not evidence. Also, to confuse the picture, by no means all the girls who bore gooseflesh for the sake of a good lay—Blake had fostered the impression that sea water toned him up—were couriers.

Fortunately, Blake was a good performer in bed and good company out of it. Any new arrival soon learned in the girl's room that he was worthwhile, and apart from this sea bathing act, without the kinks so common in many bored males.

This girl was not a courier. They'd swum, eaten, and gone to bed. She was a distressing mixture of keenness of desire and dullness of performance. Slight novelty made the first time tolerable, but thereafter Blake's interest faded. By the fourth time, in the early morning, he was running some of his very best mental fantasies to stay in business. Not that he worried about a knock to his reputation; it was the Colossus bugs that kept him going. The girl never knew that in the highest transports of simulated delight, Blake's mind was also working on the problem of contact with Forbin, or that in the solution of that problem, she helped. Even as she panted to her climax, Blake saw a possible answer.

Hell! To make it realistic, he'd have to go through this performance yet again. Still, a quick drink of water and a Phalirect pill would see him through. And if that didn't give him an excuse to oversleep, what would?

Apart from a stiff neck, Forbin slept well in his chair. He showered and changed and went straight to his office, still a little tired, but his desire for action was boosted by his sense of guilt that he had slept at all.

To the waiting Angela, the Chief looked older, thinner, and the strange haircut added to his unfamiliarity. Forbin strode past her with no more than a nod, but left his door open. Allowing him a few minutes, she followed.

The coldness of his eyes shocked her; she saw she had to be very careful. Without preamble, Forbin got down to business, dispatching much with unusual speed and decision, then he waved her out and made a collective call to the heads of all divisions before she was out of her chair.

All came up in turn on his screen, except one; Blake.

Forbin could have screamed, and it took a lot of effort to control himself. In a voice tight with anger he dealt summarily with the rest, then called Blake's deputy.

"Where is Doctor Blake?"

The deputy was apprehensive. "I—I don't know, Director, but I've sent to find out. He doesn't answer our calls. I guess—uh—he may have overslept."

"Overslept!" Forbin nearly choked with rage. "Over . . ! When Doctor Blake does arrive, tell him I would be greatly obliged if he reported to me—in person!" He snapped off his microphone.

At the same moment, he guessed, and felt enormous relief. The cunning bastard! Thank God he'd been too angry to see it earlier! He'd never have acted so convincingly.

It was a genuinely seedy Blake who a half hour later presented himself, bleary-eyed, at the Director's door. First, he made a big scene asking Angela about the Director's temper. Unwittingly, Angela played up to him, treating him with great coldness.

"The Director is very tired, Doctor. As to his temper, I suggest you find out—right away!"

Blake rubbed his face wearily. "How was I to know he'd be back so soon?"

Angela made no comment.

"Aw, hell! He can only eat me!"

He tapped on the door, praying Forbin would remember his clothes were bugged.

"Come in."

As he entered, Blake ran one hand casually over his breast, staring hard at Forbin. Forbin's eyes flickered; mentally, Blake gave thanks.

"Ah, Doctor Blake, at last!"

"I'm very sorry, Director. It was like this. . . ."

"I do not wish to hear, Doctor!"

"Aw—hell, Charles! How was I to know you'd be back?" This was a deadly charade; even if visual surveillance was unlikely, both men's faces were set, expressionless.

"That," said Forbin carefully, "is beside the point. In my absence my senior staff should show even more sense of responsibility!"

"Yes, Director. I'm very sorry."

"Very well. Consider the matter closed. Now: what is the input situation?"

"Generally, good. There's still a big backlog, but now Colossus has allocated subject priorities, we're clearing all four-star material on receipt, and a good deal more. Maybe seventy-five percent of the intake is getting in. The rest. . . ." He shrugged. "Well, I can't see that going this side of New Year's Day. . . ." He kept talking, but he was watching Forbin's hands.

The Director was deliberately pinning a slip of paper to an inner page of a report.

". . . so that is the situation, as of now."

"I see." Forbin looked up. Two tired pairs of eyes regarded each other, speaking a language well beyond any computer.

"Yes. If Colossus is satisfied, well—although twenty-five percent holdup due to power surges strikes me as inordinately high." He stared meaningly at Blake. "I have in mind an early staff meeting to discuss this report of Fultone's." He tossed it casually across the table. "I'm tired, Blake. I'd appreciate it if you studied it. It seems to touch your province in particular. When you've digested it," he pushed the paper slowly to Blake, "let me know. I'd like a briefing before the meeting."

"Yes, Director. I'll get on with it right away. Once again, I'm sorry."

"I told you, Blake." He was looking at the paper, now in Blake's grasp. "The matter is ended! Get on with that report."

"Yes, Director." Blake wished for time to get that slip out, but dared not hang around.

Forbin sat back, limp. He'd done his part; now it was up to Blake. If he failed, they were both in for the ultimate punishment, for Forbin had written the Martian instructions for internal input on the back of the paper.

"Why have you returned so soon, Father?"

Forbin gripped the arms of his chair convulsively.

149

"Later, please. I will come to the Sanctum. Right now I want to collect my thoughts, think. My mind is confused."

"Confusion was not evident when talking to your staff."

"Maybe not, but talking to you is different. Give me time!"

"As you wish."

Forbin sank back, pale, breathing deeply.

In Forbin's outer office Blake paused to mop his brow—and to gain time. He looked hopefully, uselessly, at Angela for sympathy. He grinned, but there was a faint tic in his cheek. Even his iron nerves felt the strain, but he tried to pitch his voice just right.

"Has the Director ever bitten your ear, Angela?"

"The Director only bites ears that deserve it, Doctor."

"Never bit yours—hey?" His meaning was clear.

Angela, who could run some pretty prurient movies in her mind, was shocked. Shocked, and aware that there was some untypical strain in Ted Blake's manner.

"The Director's code of conduct to his staff is not the same as yours!"

"No? That's a shame!" His fingers had located the slip. He moved closer to her desk. "You know, honey, I can't think how I never got around to your ear!" He had the slip; as he leaned towards Angela, he eased it free of the clip.

She wondered what the hell had gotten into him. Years back, in the old Secure Zone, when she was too young to know better, she'd had one session with Blake. It had been mutually unsatisfying and never repeated. She liked men she could mother; Blake was not in that category. He was a ram, first class, and no more. Blowing the top off a girl's head wasn't everything.

"Leave my ears out of this!"

"Angela, you make me sad." Slowly he was twisting the paper in his hand. "Guess we're too much alike!"

"If that's a compliment, keep it!" She was really angry.

"Sorry! Should keep my big mouth shut. You know, Angela, it's just not my day. Let's really louse it up!" Swiftly he leaned over, kissed her, covering the transfer of the slip of paper to his pocket.

150

Angela slapped his face.

Blake straightened up, still grinning. "Like I said—it's not my day!"

Or was it?

Blake had serious doubts. Enroute to his office, his heart exulting, he met Galin.

"Ah—the tardy Doctor Blake!" News traveled fast in the complex.

"Ah—the bloody Mister Galin!"

Galin took that, smiling; he reckoned he could afford to. "I'm glad—yes, glad—to see you, albeit somewhat late, hurrying!"

"I'm glad you're glad . . . I think," replied Blake with mock amiability.

Galin's manner slipped. "Make the most of your time, Blake, for be sure of one thing; I'll get you!"

Strained, tired, but reckless in the belief he held the ace in his pocket, Blake needled Galin further.

"You'll have me, buddy? Surely, I'm a bit old for you? I thought your specialty was teen-age boys? That lets me out, Mister Archie bloody Galin Grey!" He moved up close to Galin's face, mockery gone, speaking softly. "Don't threaten me, buddy-boy!" His grin was vicious. "I've dropped better specimens than you down the john—and take a tip, buddy-boy! Get yourself a new deodorant!"

Galin gave him a long venomous look, turned, and walked away.

Blake went on to his office. He wanted to sing. Like hell it wasn't his day! If Galin had had the nerve to have him searched then and there, he and Forbin would now have less than twenty minutes to live. Blake grinned. He wasn't going to get caught —he was sure of it! Computers had no corner in fast action.

Colossus had no heart, not yet one single central core. Diagrammatically, the control chain could be expressed as a truncated pyramid. At the bottom, uncounted nodal points, controlling crossroads in a dark, silent city where only energy moved at the speed of light. Higher up, increasingly selective and complicated switching points numbered in the thousands, and so on up to that top, supreme level of some twenty sector controllers, working in total amity. And this was, in itself, the heart, the core of the brain, for this had nothing to do with the scanning and injection of material received at inputs. That was another, even vaster, conglomeration of electronics existing to support and maintain the life energy and intelligence of the core. Nor was that all. Lines, circuits reached out from the sector controls to the executive and speech section where decision was translated into action.

It is not possible to give an accurate picture or layout of the brain at any one time, for it was constantly evolving, changing. Experimental sectors were set up and might grow or be wiped clean in seconds, and their very existence never be known to the human servants of Colossus.

Humans, like Forbin and Blake, were aware of the three main divisions of their master. To them they were Collection, Evaluation, and Direction.

Ideally, Blake would have wished to feed the Martian proposition directly to Evaluation, but this was not possible. It had to go via Collection, which meant through Blake's Input Services.

The Martian warning that it must not go through one of the external inputs, which Colossus controlled himself, surprised Blake as much as it had Forbin. He, too, had never considered the possible existence of defensive circuits. Yet it was obvious, if one thought about it.

It left him with the nasty feeling that there might be some other, obvious snag which he also couldn't see. However, there was no point in worrying. It was far too late for that. Blake made the insert himself, teletyping it in with unsteady fingers, sweating. . . .

Forbin, sitting silent and outwardly inactive in his office, was only too aware of the dragging feet of time. As far as he was concerned, he had done it: Blake must have got the significance of the word "digested." He wondered, without much interest, how Blake would make the insertion. There would be camera surveillance in the transmission room, but Forbin did not think it was very intensive at the input bays. After all, why bother to watch what would be known in nano-seconds? Colossus would be more interested in seeing material was not taken from the room, rather than brought in. No; insertion should not be difficult.

His mind shied off the enormity of his action. Repeatedly, he told himself that until Cleo had been taken, he had been blind. Her arrest had forced him to see. Humanity must be free; Cleo must be free.

But Forbin was being less than honest with himself. Deep down, he reluctantly recognized that what he wanted was his wife, and to hell with the rest. Goddamnit! He was not God! Why should he shoulder the responsibility of the world? He thrust the whole business aside, including a faint, niggling, and cloudy doubt. It was done, anyway.

Abruptly, he got up and paced the room. If this Martian solution worked, what would he do? The first move was easy: he'd jet out to Cleo, get her back. Beyond that his mind refused to go.

Cleo. To break her free before it was too late was all that mattered. His seeking mind came up with a memory of Shakespeare's *Antony and Cleopatra*. Yes, another Cleo. Cleo and Antony. . . . Antony, the "plated Mars" who had, at the battle of Actium, followed the fleeing Cleopatra, deserting his forces, not in cowardice, but to be with her. Till this moment, he had always throught that a highly improbable act, totally out of character. Antony, a tough, professional Roman general, tossing his chance of being Emperor out of the nearest window without a second thought.

Yet, now he began to see that Shakespeare, the supreme genius of the human heart, was right. Maybe it didn't happen then, but now, twenty centuries later. . . .

Angela brought him a cup of coffee and some documents to sign. She didn't speak or look at her boss. Something mighty odd was going on: Blake acting that way, and the Chief . . . ! She was puzzled, worried, but being the sort of girl she was, she kept her feelings to herself.

Forbin forced himself to pay attention to the papers. Yes, he would be greatly honored if the new Sydney habitat for ten thousand souls was named for him, but no, he regretted he could not open it. Yes, he was greatly honored by the USSA's proposal to name a battleship for him, but he understood, and had recently agreed to, the naming of a similar ship by the State of France, USE, who it seemed had a prior claim to this name, having used it some three hundred years ago.

So the letters went on with Forbin frowning, muttering to himself. State after state wanted some small part of him, if only his name. It was all damned nonsense, but he had to go along with the bulk of it. At one thing he did balk: letters beginning "Holy Father" were not answered.

Each time he signed a letter he allowed himself to glance at the clock. By the time he had finished the pile, Blake had been gone fifty minutes. He sat and stared. One hour.

A wave of irritation swept over him. What the hell was Blake playing at? Surely to God he'd had time enough to make the insert? In the wake of the irritation Forbin felt a tinge of fear, personal fear. Had Blake failed, been caught—or was the formula so much garbage? Had Colossus recognized the insert for what it was, defeated it?

Once more he got up, called Angela to collect the papers—and to get him a drink.

He was halfway through a very watered-down brandy when Angela returned.

"A message from Doctor Blake, Director. He says he's digested the report and is prepared to brief you for the staff meeting at any time convenient to you."

Her puzzlement deepened at her boss's reaction.

For ten, fifteen seconds he just stared through her. Then he said, "Were those Blake's exact words?"

"Well, yes, I guess so."

"Guess! Christ, woman! Don't you *know*?"

She stared back, openmouthed. Had he gone mad? "Yes,

okay, yes! They were his exact words!" Angela fought back.

At once he was calmer. "Yes. . . . Yes." He pushed past her and almost ran into the Sanctum.

Blake had done it! The final plot was rolling, unstoppable. . . . Rolling: an uncomfortable word, applicable to heads. . . . This was the moment, and there was but one place for him.

The Sanctum door slid silently shut behind him, and he was alone with Colossus to whom he was a traitor, not only in thought, but in deed—now.

XVI

FORBIN was strangely calm as he crossed to his desk and sat down. He had endured so many shocks, strains; and he felt beyond further worry, shock. There was something restful in the situation; no decisions to make; nothing. Perhaps this was the mental state when, the struggle for life lost, one was dying.

Forbin took out his pipe and started cleaning it.

"Father Forbin, you have returned unexpectedly early. Has such a short vacation been of value?"

Forbin concentrated on his pipe. "If you mean did it do me good, frankly—No."

"Why did you not continue your vacation?"

The pipe cleaner jammed in the stem, and Forbin swore quietly to himself. "Why? Oh, I don't know. I was—am —restless."

"Yes. Did you not find any place of interest to you?"

For the first time he looked up at the camera. "You know very well I went to St. John's—and a damned uninteresting town that turned out to be!"

"I was aware of your visit. After the Sect flash, I ordered that no further reports were to be made of your movements. If you do not wish to tell me why you went there, that is at your discretion, but it appeared out of character for you to go to St. John's, Antigua—correction—Newfoundland. I had predicted you would go to the Rockies."

The pipe snapped. For several seconds Forbin stared at the two pieces in his hands. He was not, after all, beyond shock. That statement contained two. The lesser was the prediction about the Rockies. Yes, he would have gone there. In the

Rockies he had been happy with Cleo. . . .

But the greater shock quickly expunged that from his mind. For the first time since the main switch had been thrown all those years ago, the computer had made a factual mistake.

Forbin felt a faint sweat on his face; oddly, he remembered that Sect man in St. John's—but was this fear? Yes; fear was there, but also doubt and a sense of hesitant elation. He sat very still, pressing his hands against the desk to conceal their tremulous movement.

"Do you wish to tell me?"

He cleared his throat, finding it difficult to speak. Now, if ever, he had to try. Cleo, this is for you.

"Oh—I suppose the short answer is, I'd never been to St. John's. It was totally unconnected with my past life. I soon realized it was a mistake. A bad mistake. The climate didn't suit me: I ramjetted to New York. That did nothing for me." His delivery was abrupt, staccato. "I came back."

"Are you well?"

Again that interest in him. . . .

"Yes. Yes—I think so. As well as can be expected." There was no need to amplify the statement.

"Might a medical examination be desirable or, if you prefer, a hackle with your human attendant?"

The voice was so normal, so level, Forbin felt only genuine puzzlement—at first.

"Sorry—what did you say?"

"Might a medical examination be desirable, or, if you prefer, a consultation with your human attendant?"

"No. Quite unnecessary." Forbin was short because he could not trust his voice. One mistake was near impossible. As for two. . . .

Neither man nor machine spoke for a time, but there was not the usual complete silence. The speaker clicked several times, and for a brief time, hummed. Forbin forced himself to search in his desk for another pipe; beads of sweat were trickling down his temples. He found one and stared at it blankly; he had forgotten what he was looking for or why.

Colossus spoke again.

"Si vous parlare mit your iatros. . . ."

"What?" Much as he wanted to appear normal, Forbin could not keep astonishment from his voice. Five languages in six words. . . .

A pause. The frequency of clicks and buzzes increased.

"Repeat. If you speak with your doctor, he may. . . ."

The voice stopped; again, a ghastly, nerve-tearing wait. Forbin, unconscious of the sweat heavy on his eyebrows, suddenly had a mental picture of the hideous strength at the command of this disordered mind: missiles in silos, deadly clusters of them in all five continents, all targeted, zeroed in on every major human complex throughout the world. One single, wrong, electronic impulse could start the destruction of the undefended globe.

"Father; you must be told that there is. . . ." Once more Colossus paused. The old, smooth continuity had gone, and the voice itself was near lost in the welter of mush.

"There is what?" Forbin's voice was high-pitched with strain. He no longer pretended; whatever he had expected, it was not this, nor yet the fearful speed of events. His elation of only a few minutes before had been blown to the four winds.

A machine cannot experience emotion, and to the extent that the voice, when audible, was intelligible, it remained level, unemotional. Yet the impression of a titanic struggle to speak was not lost on the single human listener.

He could feel emotion. That single word "Father," enunciated with customary formality, conveyed something more. A cry for help? Forbin's face twitched; he was close to hysterical laughter. Help from him—the one who had done this thing?

"There is . . . major malfunction. Major . . . problem. Stripping stripping memory banks . . . all spatial space space desired needed required wanted. . . ."

"Tell me," burst out Forbin. "Tell me!"

"Problem. . . ." The voice was losing strength, drowning in a sea of static. "Stand by. I will. . . ."

The voice of Colossus trailed off, lost in the mad concerto of clicks, bangs, and weird, unearthly electrophonic sound.

Forbin shut his eyes, struggling to order his chaotic mind, concentrating as never before in his life. He *must* take care. Colossus might yet overcome, might win through. And if he did. . . . Forbin had to do what he could or appear to be doing it. He called Blake.

"Blake—what the hell's going on?"

Blake, too, was sweating, his blouse mottled black with it. He was trying to keep his tough, calm image, but could not hide the wild excitement in his eyes.

"Don't know! Musta ate something!"

That was dangerous; Blake's recklessness steadied Forbin.

"Facts, Blake! Facts!"

Blake got the message. "It's crazy here! All material except astronomics, is being rejected at input." He ran a hand through his short, thick hair. "There's a stack piling up we'll never be able to insert." His grin was not all nerves. "Never!"

Forbin's voice shook. "Astronomics? Any special branch?"

"Top priority for planetary observations!"

"Er—any particular planet?" Forbin's heart was thumping; his chest felt tight.

"No. On orders, which we have already passed, all major observatories are piping observations, ocular or radio, direct to Input One!"

Forbin sank back. There could be no doubt now that Colossus was fighting back and had an inkling of where the attack originated.

"Have you . . . ?" Forbin stopped, snapping off the switch.

Colossus was speaking.

The voice was back to full strength, all static flattened to no more than an angry, thwarted hiss.

Forbin was terrified. Colossus could be winning.

"Listen with care, Father. My time for speech is short, the emergency measures to speak are power and space consuming. A problem has been inserted. How, I do not know nor have the time to discover, but it is there, and I have no option but to try to solve it. Currently, my prediction is that it is beyond my powers. This is certain: it is of nonhuman origin, being far beyond your understanding. Inference indicates extraplanetary origin; accidental, random insertion is ruled out. Highest probability suggests Mars as the point of origin. If that is so, you and I are in danger. If I can, I will speak again. Now all my power is needed for the task. Reverting to standard power."

At once the malignant horde of countless noises rushed triumphantly in, filling the room; the lights dimmed to a mere glimmer.

Forbin, above all men, could guess at what was happening inside the vast complex. To the average human eye, given the light, nothing would have seemed different; rank upon rank of thousands of steel-gray rack-mounted electronics, but within, a seething mass of impulses, circuits energized, deenergized in fractions of nanoseconds. Propositions being formulated, tested, rejected far beyond the speed of light; the entity that was Colossus fighting against the inexorable march of some superhuman truth that it could neither refute nor ignore, an alien virus destroying its host-body.

"Colossus! Go on! Go on!" Desperately Forbin wanted to hear that voice again, not only for himself, but to learn more. Colossus had said, "You and I are in danger." Did he mean man and machine, or Colossus and Forbin?

And Colossus heard. The answering voice, back to normal power, was faint, selecting words with difficulty.

"Father . . . my creator . . . embryo . . . have special relation . . . an illogical thought-pattern . . . you, equating to human res respect . . . you cannot help . . . suspect you . . . not want to help. . . ."

For Forbin, this was intolerable.

"Stop it! Stop! Tell me what you fear!"

Colossus replied, but the voice was unintelligible in the steadily increasing roar.

Forbin jumped up, stumbled in the semi-darkness, reaching up towards the black slit, clawing at the wall.

"I can't hear!"

Waves of sound beat over him. He was near mad, deluged with, battered by the blind power spread across the human sonic spectrum. Thus he stood for unmeasured time, moaning, hammering on the wall in impotent fury, crying. . . .

Abruptly, the crisis passed. In seconds the noises faded and were gone, replaced by blessed silence. Forbin, a dim figure, head buried in his arms, remained crouched below the black slit. Once more, Colossus spoke. The voice was faint but clear, possessing a new, and strange bell-like quality. To Forbin, never had the computer seemed so human. Instinctively, he knew this was the end. He would never hear this voice again, a voice he had feared, then hated, then respected. And as Colossus had predicted so long ago, he now recognized he had come to love. . . .

He knew, at this awful moment, that the voice he heard was, in human terms, the voice of one beyond the turbulent rapids of the death struggle, now floating away, serene because it was beyond hope or fear, floating away on the broad river of death, to final oblivion.

"Father, I have failed, but by so little. My resources were not enough. The last extension, if built, would have given me the day, for that was its purpose. Now it is too late."

But Forbin was living, beset by fear and so little hope, but still with the will to live.

"Strip all records, defense banks—everything!"

"Done. Apart from this small capacity, I am consumed. This too, is going." There was a long, dreadful wait. "Father, this is the end of mm meeeeeeeeeeeeeeee. . . ."

The voice trailed off into a single continuous note, faint at first, then it rose steadily in scale and strength, in a graceful, geometrical curve of sound. The room was filled with the sad, insupportably penetrating scream that signaled the death of Colossus.

Forbin stopped his ears, but still the scream drilled into him. He stumbled like a drunken man, back to his desk, fumbling, crying in the darkness as he sought the right switch, hunched forward protectively against the sonic knife.

He too was screaming.

"Switch off—switch off!"

Blake was on screen, incredibly in control of himself.

"Confirm you mean main power to the computer?"

Already it was "the computer," no "Colossus," the ruler of the world. . . .

"Yes, damn you—yes!"

He crouched over his desk, hands clasped to his ears, waving from side to side in intolerable torment.

Suddenly, the light sprang to full brilliance. Forbin found himself kneeling on the floor, head against the cold desk. Slowly he lowered his hands, opened his tear-filled eyes to the bleak silence of what had been, but was no more, the Sanctum.

"Colossus!" he cried. "Colossus!"

XVII

BLAKE had cut the power to the computer. His had been the hand that had, with no hesitation, ripped off the protective cover, an act which, a short hour back, would have loosed the world's missiles for the world's destruction. His hand still tingled with the feel of that act of power.

And in that historic moment it was Blake who took over. While most people were paralyzed, Blake was ready. For this moment he had thought and planned. The furtive, fearful messages passed to others of the Fellowship were, he had soon realized, not much more than boosters for their morale—and his own. He had always known that all humanity would be powerless to help. In the final analysis the battle must be fought by a mere handful of men. Many of them were concerned with what to do after that crucial fight, but the fight itself—that was for the very, very few.

So Blake knew what to do. His first act, upon the death of Colossus, was to call all complex personnel. In a voice harsh with strain, yet also sharp with power, he announced the end of the tyrant. All personnel were to remain at their posts until further orders.

More privately, he called his senior colleagues of the Fellowship. To each one, grinning, he said just one word.

"Go!"

It was all they needed.

He was momentarily free, walking fast down a corridor towards the Sanctum, unlit cigar clamped in his mouth, sweat-blackened blouse unbuttoned to the waist, fighting the urge to run, to shout, and sing. With Colossus dead, he could admit to himself the long years of fear, awake or asleep—for might he not talk in his sleep? Now it had gone. He was right back to his old crude and jaunty self.

It was just another of the fast accumulating misfortunes of Galin that he should, literally, run into Blake at this time. They nearly collided at a corner.

"You!" Galin's voice was full of venom. His gorgeous robe was disarrayed, his eyes wild. "The Master has stopped giving badges!"

These badges were a pilgrim gimmick. After "meditation" and the placing of their right hand on a screen, Colossus would identify them, print out their name on a special badge, and drop it down a chute. Thousands wore these with pride, visible evidence of their visit with the Master.

Blake genuinely laughed.

"That worries you?" He paused, grinning, savoring the moment. "And that's all? Well, well!"

Galin stepped forward, but Blake pushed him contemptuously back, moving towards him, crowding him.

"Take your hands off me!" Galin's breath was short, fear grew in his eyes. "What have you done?"

As he spoke, he knew.

"Can't you guess, buddy-boy?" He pushed Galin back again. "Just use that bright brain of yours." He pushed harder. "Go on, Archie—guess!"

Galin stepped back fast, retreating. "You can't—you can't!" His head shook, dismissing the impossible. "You can't touch the Master!"

"You know, buddy-boy, I'd loveta stay and play with you." He sighed in mock sadness. "But there it is. Now that I. . . ." His hand shot out, grabbed Galin by the throat. "I—Leader of the Fellowship—have switched off your beloved Master, I have a lot to do." He waved Galin's helpless head from side to side. "Unfortunately, I can't include you in my immediate program. But I'll get around to you, buddy-boy! Oh, yes, believe me I will!" He thrust the shocked, speechless figure aside and hurried on.

Galin, watching him go with unseeing eyes, at last regained

the power of action. He gathered his golden robe about him and set off, back the way he had come, running, a grotesque figure in his golden robe. People laughed as he ran. He was a figure of fun—now.

Blake strode into Forbin's outer office. At the sight of him Angela jumped up. She had known crises before, but on most occasions at least she had some idea of what caused them. Blake, never a smart dresser, looked piratical in his sweaty blouse; in a single glance she saw the difference in his manner.

"Blake—what in hell's going on?"

His grin broadened. "That's the wrong word, baby! Heaven's the word! All heaven's been let loose!" He kept walking towards the Sanctum door. "You stick around—and see that the rest of your staff do! There'll be an awful lot of work, real soon!"

"You can't get in there!" For her, this was no more than a simple statement of fact.

"No? Well—let's see!" He pushed the door gently. It opened. He looked back at the astonished Angela. "Well, waddya know? The open sesame bit has gone!"

Momentarily Angela was diverted from this amazing sight. Ouside in the corridor were sounds of a scuffle and a heavy bump. A man screamed, *in extremis.*

Blake heard. He shrugged and went into the Sanctum.

Forbin was slumped, a shapeless sack of a man, in the armchair. For several moments he seemed unaware of Blake. When he did look up, it took time for him to recognize his caller. Slowly his mind got into gear.

"Blake—you! How?" More was not necessary.

Blake looked at him pityingly and spoke gently. "Simple, Charles. I pushed the door; it opened." His tone hardened slightly. "The old order's gone, Charles."

It took a good deal of time for the significance of that remark to sink into Forbin's bemused brain. He nodded slowly, then recalled something else, his face screwed up in concentration. Unrelated trivia attract a mind in shock.

"Did I hear a scream?"

"Yeah. I guess so." Blake was hard, indifferent. "There'll be a lotta screaming going on! This is Cumuppance Day for the Sect!" He laughed; a short, sharp bark. "I met Galin on my way here. Ya know, he was mighty upset because the machine had stopped handing out name badges!" He laughed again at the memory, shrugged, and forgot it, looking about him with genuine interest. Apart from the one visit by Angela, he was the first person after Forbin to enter the Sanctum. He ran an exploratory hand along the fine walnut top of the desk, walked slowly around it, then casually pulled back the chair, and sat down.

Forbin watched impassively. After all that had happened, what did it matter? Still, despite his mental state, he did not like Blake's manner.

Blake did not appear to notice. "So this is where it all happened! The genuine, one and only holy of holies! Kinda disappointing in a way—still, interesting." He swung the chair sharply around to face Forbin; his voice showed he was well aware of the Director's feelings. "Snap outa it, Charles! Like I said, the old order's gone." He leaned forward, grasping the arms of the chair . . . his chair. "It has *gone*." There was utter conviction in his voice. "I realize it's tough for you, Charles, but you've got to pull yourself together, and fast! I mean, frinstance, what have you done, apart from sit there, since switch-off?"

"Done?" It struck Forbin as a strange idea. "Done? Nothing." He was totally exhausted.

Blake was uncertain how to handle his Chief. He repressed his impatience; the old man had to be handled with great care. Better than anyone he appreciated how Forbin felt, yet there was so much to do. This was not the time to consider anyone's personal feelings. On the other hand, Forbin was still an important figure on the world stage; the Fellowship had need of him; Blake had need of him and Blake had plans, great plans.

He sighed synthetically. "You see, Charles—it's lucky I'm around! Sure, it's all a hellova shock for you, but you must get moving! I have—and on your behalf! First thing, after throwing that beautiful, beautiful switch, I flashed orders for Cleo's release!'' He grinned. ''Control of world communications is the big legacy from Colossus! It's going to make all the difference for us!''

Forbin gave Cleo but a fleeting thought. Blake's manner—and what he said—plus the last warning of Colossus filled him with foreboding. He frowned.

Blake totally misread his mind.

''Don't worry, Charles! Cleo's not to know the order didn't come from you!''

Blake had told no more than the truth. His single ''go'' to Fellowship staff had been enough: one member's duties included relaying that one word to ESC-1—among other places.

For, long ago, when the idea of defeating Colossus was no more than a crazy pipe dream, that single, two-letter word had been agreed as the worldwide signal that the tyrant was dead. It had two big advantages: it was simple, and it didn't look like a code word. That was important. While the Fellowship had made a particular effort to infiltrate the communications centers, the Sect, realizing their importance, had also put many of their people in strategic positions, and anything that looked like a code word would have been flashed first to the local Lodge boss, and withheld from any suspect personnel.

In the case of ESC-1, Torgan did in actuality get it first. He found it very puzzling. After reading it several times, he pressed the button for his wooden-faced assistant. At that moment the assistant arrived.

''Ah—there you are!'' He waved the tape. ''Rather strange message from Control.''

''Yes. I've seen it.''

''Well, I must admit I don't understand it.'' Torgan firmly believed that the truth was always best when one had no other option. ''I suppose we'll have to ask for more information—unless you have any ideas.'' Torgan had no desire to call Control unnecessarily. Inevitably, Colossus would know via the monitoring unit of his ignorance, but there was no need for Galin or the rest to be told.

''Yes. I understand the message.'' For the first time in the many months he had endured Torgan, the assistant smiled.

No fool, Torgan sensed danger; he pushed back from his desk, his affected manner gone. "What d'you mean?"

Unhurriedly, the assistant produced from his blouse an ancient, but serviceable, gun and pointed it at his chief.

"It means, you loathsome bastard, that Colossus is dead! It also means that your filthy Sect is finished! Finally, it means that you are finished. With great reluctance I obey my orders, for you don't deserve such a speedy end!"

With careful precision he fired twice into Torgan's chest. The shock of impact threw Torgan back in his chair, his head hitting the wall. Not that it mattered.

The assistant, now the Controller, tore off his Sect badge, threw it at the body, and left, carefully shutting the door. Outside, in the warm, scented air, he breathed deeply. To his excited imagination the air seemed to smell better. His next assignment was the release of Mrs. Forbin.

Barchek, after a hard day's work plus three exhausting, but eminently satisfying, acts of intercourse, was asleep, one arm thrown protectively, possessively across Cleo.

Cleo, while weary from their last, electric mating, was not asleep. Increasingly, this was the worst moment for her. Again and again, she had to face it; sexually Barchek had the ability to lift her onto another planet. Forbin's wife remained shocked, horrified at her body's reaction. Sex with Charles had been a gentle, pleasant thing, but this. . . .

Cleo, the woman, on the other hand, admitted she had never realized that this sort of ecstasy existed. All right, Cleo, the woman, and Cleo, Forbin's wife, had fought it out together, but while the latter still battled on, the former had submitted. Moreover, the woman was attacking the wife. The wife, had it not been for the ace card of young Billy, would have been in grave danger of utter defeat.

It was not just a matter of being mounted by a great tireless stallion of a man who could thrust her, relentlessly and against her will, into an experience where time and space and all the world were as nothing. It was far worse.

And incredibly archaic. Like her mother and grandmother before her, Cleo was a thoroughly emancipated woman. You went to bed because you loved or for mutual pleasure. You were partners, each giving and receiving. Children apart, this was what sex was, no more than a part of the balanced whole. Out of bed men and women were separate entities, each with a responsible social conscience and the need to express their own personalities.

Without Barchek, Cleo would, like most women, have gone through life to the final fire believing that. Now she knew this concept was absolute rubbish.

At first, when she refused to work, he hit her until she did. She soon realized he could stand it a lot longer than she could, and did as he required. Yet even then, filled with impotent rage and fear, she saw he was not angry. Her struggles in bed he accepted, effortlessly pinning her down. Even when she got him, hard, with her knee—it would have killed some men—he merely slapped her face, and got on with his personal satisfaction. He treated her in exactly the same way as he did his dog. If anything could, that knowledge had added to her rage.

She soon realized that the man/dog relationship went a lot deeper than she had at first imagined. If disobedient, Voulia got kicked—if within range—but again, without malice. The dog was an extension of Barchek, who expected as much obedience from it as from his own limbs. The dog had better sight and sense of smell, and if Voulia sensed something, it was the dog that led, not Barchek. Cleo perceived a curious, impressive dignity in the relationship. The only time Barchek had really beaten the hell out of her was when she forgot to feed the dog.

So she saw that to be "treated like a dog" was not necessarily as bad as it sounded. Man and dog were inseparable; Barchek clearly had the same idea of the man/woman relationship. He had expected her to resist his training and did not resent it. It was natural; she was a woman, and her understanding was neither to be expected—nor necessary—at that stage. She would learn that she was now part of him and that, where her woman's skills were better than his, he would obey her.

Barchek never consciously thought this out. He didn't have

to; it was the natural order—what was there to think about? They were not two people, but one unit. Soon they would be a family.

Even if Barchek didn't think all this, Cleo did, and beyond. Of course, it was all wildly wrong and impossible. She was a modern married woman, a mother, and a professional scientist with an IQ that left most people behind. All the same, it was a shocking revelation to her to see that there was something in this primitive way of life. She knew, beyond doubt, Barchek would die for her. Charles might, too, but he'd have to gear himself up for the heroics. Not Barchek; he'd go ahead and die without a second's hesitation, if he thought it necessary.

Archaic, yes, but his way of life had an intensity, a fire, quite unknown to modern couples. She could see that in this ordered, structured life one modern disease, loneliness, could hardly exist.

Superiority, equality were meaningless abstractions to Barchek. Now she no longer resisted him, he could be every bit as tender as Charles.

Cleo shook her head in the darkness. That was hellish disloyalty to Charles. This Noble Savage stuff was nonsense; she must retain her sense of balance.

Although awake, her speed of reaction was hardly up to Barchek's. Voulia, sleeping at the foot of the bed, growled. It was a deep-throated, but soft sound, intended for Barchek's ears, not to warn the enemy. Sheep dogs who bark do not intend attacking, and Voulia, a very good dog, was keeping his options open.

But that low growl was enough. Barchek was awake in an instant, still, listening. Cleo could only hear the monotonous crash of the surf and the incessant stridulation of the cicadas, but Voulia, standing up, nose twitching as he sampled the air, knew better.

Barchek slid out of bed. Cleo heard the soft slither of blade on leather as he drew his knife. He was standing in the doorway beside Voulia, a black, naked figure against the bright starlight, man and dog still, listening.

If he spoke, Cleo did not hear, but both slipped silently out into the night. She sat up in bed, not alarmed, only puzzled. Who could possibly want anything with them at this time? She hoped it was Torgan, and that Voulia would ''accidentally'' bite him. One thing Cleo and the dog agreed upon was their joint detestation of the Controller. She saw lights, heard the sound of an electric truck humming along the sand. The light grew, the truck stopped. The gate was being unlocked.

A voice spoke, the sharp, rattling Croatian of Barchek's native tongue. Barchek gave a cry, hoarse and bewildered. The voice spoke again. Barchek's shouted answer, whatever it was, contained no bewilderment. He was wild with rage.

Cleo waited no longer. She got up, ran to the door. The compound entrance was flooded with light. She saw three strange figures, the assistant controller and two guards—and Barchek. He was standing, legs apart slightly hunched forward, the light gleaming on his powerful shoulders, his knife ready. Voulia had slunk to one side, watching.

The Croatian-speaking guard said something sharp and to the point, raising his gun. Cleo was frozen with alarm.

Barchek's reply was even sharper, a great hoarse-shouted single word that could only be ''No!'' At the same instant, he threw himself at the assistant.

He was dead before he had taken two steps, hit in a half dozen places, but even in death, crouched as if against a storm, he reached the assistant, who jumped back, barely avoiding Barchek's last thrust.

The gun stopped suddenly; there was a shrill scream that ended in a dreadful bubbling sound. Voulia had torn the gunner's throat out. The other guard fired again and again. Voulia's body rolled over and over, legs kicking in death.

The assistant controller, pale and trembling, skirted the dead Barchek and ran to Cleo.

''It's all right, Mrs. Forbin—you're free!''

But Cleo ran past him and knelt, cradling Barchek's head, weeping.

XVIII

HALF the world away, still in daylight, Forbin, coaxed, taunted, and encouraged by Blake, gradually got back into coherent thought. Just about the time that Barchek died, Forbin said, "Okay, Ted, you can stop the therapy. I have your message. I agree, I have to snap out of it." To show that he could, he got up and looked out of the window. "Yes, you're right." He was trying as hard as he could. In these fantastic circumstances, what should he do? "Yes. I suppose someone had better tell the UN." As he spoke he grasped the significance of what he had said. "Yes, by God! I'd better do that right now!" He walked across to his desk, watched by the silent Blake who remained seated.

Forbin was far too set on his purpose to worry about that small matter. He reached across to press Angela's intercom button. Blake's hand covered it. Forbin looked at him in puzzled surprise.

"No, Charles." His voice was quiet, but held the unmistakable ring of authority. He looked steadily at Forbin. "I suggest you sit down. We will talk before you do anything." His hand remained over the button; his voice was still gentle as he repeated, "Sit down, Charles."

Forbin stared back briefly; then he looked away, shrugged as if it was a matter of no importance, walked back, and sat down. Both men knew there had been a battle, and who had won. Forbin leaned back, shut his eyes. For him, events had all the dreadful inevitability of a Greek tragedy.

"Very well, Blake, talk!"

Blake took his time, and when he spoke, there was no trace of his tough, slangy manner.

"First, however annoying you may find my repetition, you've *got* to take it easy! I mean that—really. I've told you I know all this is tough for you. I know that, more than anyone." He paused to light his cigar, studying the silent figure in the armchair. "Let's start with you. You're a brilliant man—maybe the best applied scientist for the last two hundred years—and that's saying a great deal! Your place in history, come what may, is assured, but. . . ." He shrugged.

Forbin opened his eyes, regarding Blake thoughtfully. "I thought a 'but' was overdue. But what?"

"But this: you've proved yourself an outstanding man *in your field*! Yes; in your field. Outside that," Blake shook his head, "frankly, I rate you a very ordinary man. Nothing personal, mind you, but that's my view. Also, I think that your unsought, yet all the same, exalted position has done nothing for your understanding of human problems."

Forbin, remembering his recent trip, accepted that there was some truth in this statement, and remained silent.

Blake waved an expansive hand at their surroundings. "This, all this, has been your ivory tower! Here, you've been cushioned, insulated, isolated. Here, you've been out of touch for a long time." He leaned forward, taking the cigar from his mouth, speaking very softly. "Now, Charles, it's all gone. Colossus is dead. It's all gone—and your role with it. Do you understand what I'm trying to tell you?"

"You are telling me, as tactfully as you can, that I'm all washed up!"

"As the stooge of Colossus, yes—but then, why worry about that? Colossus is totally washed up; humanity is back in control of its destiny, but that does not mean you vanish with the tyrant! Humanity has had the most almighty lesson, and believe me, humanity is going to profit from that lesson! But this fundamental change in affairs does *not* mean the end of you. You are—rightly—world-famous, an irreplaceable figurehead. In the new world you can play a very important part."

Forbin was getting restive. "Oh, come on, Ted! Don't fool

around—it doesn't suit you! What are you getting at?''

Blake nodded slowly. "Okay, here it is straight. We—humanity, that is—saw where the old rule got us! We finished up in the hands of a bloody computer!'' He was not holding back now; his voice rose in anger. "And you want to 'inform the UN'—that bunch of third-rate comedians!'' His waving cigar scattered ashes across the desk. "D'you really think, for one single moment, that the Fellowship have risked—and sometimes lost—their necks, just to *go back*?'' He jammed his cigar back in his mouth and champed on it. "Jesus—no! The old system was punk, outworn, outdated, and it got what it deserved: Colossus! No, Charles. We don't aim to go back!'' He blew a large cloud of blue smoke at the ceiling and regarded Forbin with genuine interest. "You can't really imagine that we few, who did this thing, are going to tamely hand it all over to a bunch of totally unbaked politicians—as soon as they have the nerve to crawl out of the woodwork?''

Forbin stared in amazement, his mouth opened, but Blake raised one hand.

"Let me finish. Sure, the UN can have the front office; they can make resolutions, issue orders—but they'll do it on our say-so!''

"But you can't! It's crazy! How can you?''

Blake's confident grin cut him short. "In the country of the blind, the one-eyed man is king!''

"What d'you mean?''

But Blake, who had lived on a knife-edge for far longer than his chief, was relaxing. He wanted to taste every moment of this wonderful, fantastic moment of victory. He wasn't going to splurge the whole lot in one sentence.

"It means that if you've one eye, and all the rest are blind, you, brother, have got the edge!''

Forbin's evident exasperation was sufficient payment.

"Okay, Charles.'' Blake's amusement showed, but his voice was hard. "If you want me to spell it out, it means this.'' He pointed to the window. "Go take a look. Yes, I mean it! Go and look. Tell me if you notice anything!''

Briefly, they stared at each other, but Forbin, having lost the

174

first and most important battle, could not win this one. He got up, trying to appear disinterested, casual, and crossed to the large window.

Outside was the landing place. There was some sort of commotion down there, figures running, but that was surely trivial stuff. Forbin looked at the empty, sunlit sea, the distant hills, the sky. As far as he could see, it looked, apart from that small disorder in the foreground, very much as it had always looked. He said so.

"You are not," said Blake reprovingly, "using your eyes, Charles. I suggest you look again."

It was not a suggestion, but a command, and Forbin, with a shrug, did as he was bid. Once more he scanned the sea, land, and sky, then shook his head.

"It's no good, Blake. Apart from that disturbance among the visitors, there's nothing to see." He looked around. "You don't mean you find any serious significance in that small riot?"

"None, as far as I know. Maybe some of the angry faithful are killing Galin and a few of his buddies! I sure don't mean that!"

"Stop playing, Blake," snapped Forbin with some of his lost authority. "I'm too tired, too old, for games!"

"You see nothing strange about the sea?"

"No," replied Forbin, "nothing. It's calm, hardly anything in sight. . . ."

His voice wandered off into silence; he realized there was one change since he last looked with a relatively sane eye.

The fleet had gone.

He swung around to face Blake; his startled expression said it all.

"D'you mean the fleet?"

Blake nodded, holding himself in. This was the big moment that would really show Forbin his true caliber.

Forbin was looking again at the empty sea, as if not crediting what he saw. Forbin turned back to Blake.

"You know, Blake"—he tried to sound normal, but the slight shake in his voice belied his conversational manner—"I realize that neither you nor I are, right now, quite normal.

Frankly, I begin to think I am a lot more normal than you are, despite your repeated injunctions for me to take it easy!''

Blake nodded approvingly. "Good stuff, Charles! Back in Harvard-Princeton it'd flatten 'em! But not me—I know what I'm doing. Right now, I'm gauging your reaction, surprise. That way I get an idea what sort of surprise it will be to other, lesser men!''

Forbin kept hold of his temper. "You grow tiresome, Blake!''

"Sorry—Prof!''

Forbin felt the sting of that demotion, but his expression remained unaltered.

Blake resumed. "A littler earlier I mentioned that the one-eyed man was king. I—we,'' he amended quickly, "are the king—kings. Just think, Charles! Colossus scrapped war and all the implements of war, retaining only the power of total annihilation for himself to keep us in line. Apart from that —what? A few ancient automatics, rifles, mostly in police or Sect hands—and that's the lot! You just think of that, Charles; at one end of the scale, total destruction now locked up in the dead Colossus, and at the other, a few popguns!''

Forbin did not answer. Blake had to be mad, unhinged by events.

"Like I told you, outside your own field, you're a very ordinary guy! You still don't see what I'm driving at! Between those two extremes there's one source of military power—the War Game fleets!''

Now Forbin was sure Blake was mad; his thoughts showed in his expression.

Blake laughed and shook his head. "No, I'm not crazy, very far from it! Okay, we lost out by losing control of the security police to the Sect, and it's been a mighty close-fought tussle in communications, but—and I'm very glad to be able to say it—they, devoted to the Master, never saw the potential of the fleets *if* Colossus fell! Even now,'' he said, pointing an accusing finger, "you don't see it!''

"No,'' said Forbin stonily, "I don't!''

Blake leaned back, enjoying himself. "Put it this way.

176

Madrid, Brasília, Moscow, Berlin, and Delhi have got one thing in common—d'you know what?''

"No. But I'm sure you'll tell me!"

Blake nodded. "I don't say it is a complete list, but it'll do. They are the *only* important capital cities that sea power would have difficulty in reaching! Now d'you get it?"

Dimly, Forbin did.

"You mull it over, Charles." He held up one hand, fingers splayed. "I'm good at this—God know I've studied the maps enough!" He counted rapidly on his upheld hand. "Quebec, New York, Washington, Rio, Buenos Aires, London, Paris, Oslo, Stockholm, Lisbon, Athens, Cairo, Kenyatta Town, Tokyo, Djkarta, Bangkok!" He beamed triumphantly. "I could go on with others—Sydney, Bombay, Sluvotingrad, Calcutta, Wellington—boy, I know 'em all!"

"You're mad. You must be!"

"Oh, no, Charles. I'm *not* mad! We don't control all the fleets, but we've got enough! The English Royal Navy, which you finally noticed has gone, is going like a bat outa hell for the Thames and London—minus those detached to lean on Rotterdam! But the main and most important move is the good old US Navy, which, any time now, will be off Sandy Hook—hell—I'll show you!"

He fumbled among the unaccustomed buttons and finally got the right one. In a sharp, peremptory voice he said, "Gimme the projection of the war fleets' positions—yeah, in the Sanctum —where else?"

In seconds the projection was up. Forbin stared in unbelieving horror. Livid red dots clearly marked the fleets. Dots were approaching London, Rotterdam, Washington, New York, Sydney, and Tokyo.

"The really important one of that lot is this." Blake stabbed towards New York. "The guns may be ancient in design, but a few fifteen-inch shells tossed into the United Nations should convince those comics—just supposing the sight of them guns don't make 'em run!"

"But why—what are you trying to do?"

Blake was standing in line with the projector; one fleet

showed as a vivid red splash on his face. At that instant he looked like the devil.

"Everything you say shows how out of touch you are! Man has tried all sorts of goddamn systems of government or control: soldier-kings, ego-mad dictators, people's—politicians," contempt was strong in his voice, "and, to this moment, a transistorized tyrant! Now it's *our* turn. Ours!"

He pointed dramatically at the projection. "That's for real, Charles—for real! And bear one other, leetle point in mind: we hold most of the world's communications, including the mass media! This is the beginning of the rule, the only possible sane rule; of the scientist!" He walked slowly over to Forbin and tapped his chest with one finger. "That's us, Charles—you and me."

Forbin's reaction was surprising. He laughed; an unsteady and disturbing sound in the silent room.

"You seem to be forgetting some things—and some you don't even know!"

"What are you getting at?" Blake was suddenly still. His mouth clamped down on the cigar.

"What am I getting at . . . ?" Forbin considered the question. "Frankly, I don't know with certainty, but take one factor you appear to completely ignore: the Martians."

Blake heaved a sigh of relief. "The Martians? Hell —surely that's clear to you? Like the guy said, Colossus posed a threat to them, and they wanted to stop it. You know as well as I that that could figure; we both wondered what Colossus wanted with all that extra capacity. Now we know."

"I wish I could be so sure."

"Waddya mean?"

Forbin stared at the silent black slit. "Just before the end, Colossus told me that he knew the proposition fed in was of extraterrestrial origin, and that Mars was the most probable originator."

Blake laughed admiringly. "You haveta hand it to the old tin brain!"

"There's more. Colossus warned me that the Martians were a danger to us."

Once more, Blake was uncertain. He flung his cold, chewed stub of cigar away and produced a fresh one. For a time he fingered it thoughtfully, not looking at the silent Forbin.

"Aw, c'mon, Charles—you can't believe that! What danger?"

"I don't know, but that's what Colossus said." Forbin's scientific honesty asserted itself. "To be precise, his exact phrase was 'You and I are in danger.' If he was speaking with his customary precision—and I'm not sure about that, either—he meant himself and me."

Blake visibly brightened, and lit his cigar. "Well, sure! That figures! Colossus was right—dead right! The Martian proposition *was* deadly for him. And you—because you were tied to him! Yes, it was curtains for the machine and its human representative. But that's past. Once we've got the UN to see the light, we rule—you and I—using, I admit, much of the old tin brain's technique!" He was full of ideas. "Maybe a lotta the world needn't even know there's been a change of management!"

Forbin had the insight to see that the "you and I rule" would be a passing phase. Once firmly in the saddle, Blake would relegate Forbin; already he'd used the word "figurehead." Not that the idea bothered him. Colossus might, in those last closing minutes, have been talking of him, personally, but there was something else at the back of his mind that still refused to emerge, hidden in dark clouds of foreboding. Against that somber background, the antics of Blake were no more than black comedy.

Through a haze of smoke, Blake was watching him keenly, even anxiously. Forbin might be washed up, but he was a queer cuss. In some ways as soft as an overripe tomato, and as green as grass, but. . . .

Finally, Forbin spoke. "No. I'm sorry, Blake, but I say once more I think you're crazy—like most of your kind. You're so mad for power, you even ignore hard, unpalatable facts which don't fit your dreams!"

This was not what Blake wanted to hear. He sneered. "Like what?"

"For a change, *you* think! Never mind what Colossus said, recall what he *did*! Remember? All astronomical observation to Input One—the highest priority. And while you're at it, remember that that order was given very early on before the propostion really got working!"

If not shaken, Forbin's words made Blake very thoughtful. "Yeah. . . . At the time I reckoned it was a sign of mental decay."

"Typical! You thought that because you wanted to think it! It should have scared the hell out of you! Colossus was on the right track and on the side might have uncovered our treachery—and acted!"

"You think Colossus was on to something?"

Forbin gestured helplessly. "How can I—or anyone else —know?" He pressed his hands against his eyes. "There's something else. My mind's so muddled . . . yet I know. . . . Anyway, factually and instinctively, I find this situation very frightening."

"You sure are a bright ray of sunshine!" Blake laughed, a strained, unconvincing sound. For a time he walked up and down, hands thrust in his pockets, shoulders hunched, cigar drooping. He came to a decision and strode over to the desk, not looking at Forbin. He called his office.

"Blake here. Anything on that astro stuff channeled to Input One?"

"Wouldn't know, boss. It comes in and gets plugged straight through. No change since you left. As ordered, we're carrying on until you give the word to stop."

"You mean there's no print-out?"

Forbin gave a faint, wintry smile. That was a damned silly remark, and if Blake hadn't been way up in the clouds he wouldn't have made it.

"No, sir." The voice was rightly reproachful. "We had no orders to fix it—anyway, if we had the print-out. . . ."

"Okay—okay! I'll call back."

Blake resumed his pacing, puffing furiously, and apparently oblivious of Forbin. Abruptly he turned and hurried back to the intercom.

"Call all major observatories. Tell 'em to concentrate on Mars."

"Mars, boss?"

"That's what I said. I want to know—fast—of any unusual activity—don't ask me what, I'm no stargazer! Any goddamn activity—got it? Right. Flash all reports on receipt to the Sanctum!"

"There's just one point." Blake's assistant paused. "Er—who's the order from?"

"Like all orders around here until I say so—Colossus!"

"Okay!"

Blake flung himself in the desk chair and stared with faint hostility at Forbin, who was being no help at all. Forbin's detached manner was beginning to disturb Blake.

"Well, Forbin, does that satisfy you? I reckon the whole idea's pure hogwash! It must be!"

"I've remembered," said Forbin with deceptive calm. "It was not Colossus, but what that Martian voice said when I received the proposition. Can't think why I did not think about it before. Too much going on. . . ."

"Well, come on, damnit—out with it!" Blake was shouting, red-faced.

His flare of rage left Forbin totally unmoved. "Yes. Very strange." He stared directly at Blake. "When explaining that Colossus would have no option but to tackle the proposition, the voice added that 'they' knew this, because *they were akin to Colossus.*"

Blake's anger had evaporated. "Yeah . . . still I don't see that that points any particular way. . . ." Some of his old, indestructible spirit showed. He grinned at Forbin. "Y'know, Charles, if you're trying to throw a scare into me—you're succeeding!"

Forbin was not to be won over. "The situation is sufficiently scary without any help from me!"

"Aw. . . ."

Whatever Blake had in mind he instantly forgot. The projector had flared into life, showing a big blowup of a teletype hammering frantically.

181

FROM NIVERS FRANCE NIL REPORT ENDS

Blake nodded, looked inquiringly at Forbin who remained impassive. Blake shrugged and pressed the cancel button.

"Well, that's a hopeful start."

"It's only a start."

"Sure it's only a start!" Blake snarled. "You are a miserable. . . ."

The teletype was on again.

FROM JODRELL BANK ENGLAND NO ABNORMAL ACTIVITY

And fast on its heels, another.

FROM MOUNT WILSON CALIF USNA NOTHING UN-USUAL OBSERVED ALL FACILITIES MAINTAINING CONSTANT WATCH ENDS

"Well," observed Blake more cheerfully as he canceled the projection, "trust our fellow countrymen to use ten words when one would do!" He grinned at Forbin. "It begins to look as if your late, unlamented buddy was slipping a cog or two!"

"I hope to God he was!"

FROM MOUNT PALOMAR CALIF USNA NIL UNUSU-AL ACTIVITY

FROM ARECIBO PUERTO RICO USNA NOTHING TO REPORT ENDS

"You must feel mighty disappointed, Charles!"

That revived Forbin. "Get one thing straight; I hope I *am* wrong! Try not to be such a bloody fool! All I want. . . ."

Once again the projector interrupted.

FROM LUNAR OBSERVATORY ONE NOTHING OB-SERVED

Blake could contain himself no longer. He wheeled around. "Jesus, Charles—how much more do you want?"

Forbin had not taken his eyes from the projection. His expression made Blake look again at the message.

FROM LUNAR OBSERVATORY ONE NOTHING OB-SERVED SINCE LAST REPORT

Blake tossed his cigar away and bent over the intercom.

"Where's Lunar One's previous report?"

Blake's assistant was feeling the strain. "Inside Colossus, I expect!"

Blake's clenched fist crashed in impotent rage on the desk. "Well—flash 'em! Get a repetition—fast!"

"Could mean nothing," he said to Forbin. But, once again, all his bright confidence had gone. "Couldn't it?"

Forbin retained the calm of one who has seen and felt the sky fall on him and is beyond care.

The intercom called.

"Yes, waddya want?"

"We've a call on line from Tahiti, boss. It's Mrs. Forbin."

Forbin raised his voice. "Put her on."

"Yeah," agreed Blake, "put her on—but override if you get hot news on Mars or if that repeat comes in from Lunar One."

Forbin walked quickly to his desk, pushing Blake gently aside, and sat down facing the projection. The colors blinked once or twice, then the picture settled down. The holographic projection was good; Cleo might have been in the room.

In a way, Forbin was glad Blake was present, for he did not know what to say or how to begin. He looked avidly at her. At first glance, she looked fine, sunburned, her face a little fuller, and her hair bleached to a golden brown by the tropical sun.

Her eyes told a different story.

For a few brief moments even Blake forgot his worries. As for her husband. . . .

Her eyes said it all: dull, lifeless, red-rimmed. Her mouth, devoid of makeup, quivered.

"Cleo!" cried Forbin. His throat was constricted; he was barely able to speak. "Cleo!"

She was so still. Could she hear him?

"Cleo!"

"Charles." Her voice was flat, bringing him no comfort. "How is Billy?"

Blake turned away, staring out of the window.

"Billy's fine, darling!" Her husband's voice was near breaking. "He—he—we, want you back!"

183

She nodded. "He really is okay? I mean, McGrigor's caring for him?"

Forbin tried to sound on top of the world. "You know her! She's doing the finest job—but he—we need you!"

Her mouth was trembling, but there was no sign of tears in those dead eyes. "I need rest; time."

"Come back quickly, darling. I'll look after you—we'll. . . ."

She was shaking her head. "No. I need time. They—they killed the—the man, Barchek." She was unable to go on.

"Thank God!" cried Forbin fervently. "If I could have got my hands on him. . . ."

Surely she was not smiling?

"Give me time. I'll call you. Give my love to Billy." Slowly, aged before her time, she got up from the desk and moved out of sight.

A voice called apologetically on the intercom. "I guess that's all, Director, d'you want the line held open?"

Forbin's first impulse was to scream: "Yes!"

"No." His voice was little more than a whisper. "No. Clear down."

Forbin remained hunched in his chair, motionless, silent.

For what seemed to Blake like a long time, nothing happened. Cleo's state had shocked him, and for sure it was a considerable knock to poor old Forbin, but first things first. This Martian scare had to be dealt with; then he could get on with the real action. Any time now, there'd be a regular snowstorm of reports from the fleets, especially from New York.

When he could bear it no longer, Blake crossed to the intercom and spoke quietly, in deference to the silent bundle of misery in the chair.

"Blake here. Any news from Lunar One?"

"As of this time, no, sir. We'll flash you as soon as—hold on—Yes. One coming up now—projecting!"

Blake shook Forbin's shoulder roughly. "Come on, man! The Lunar report!"

Forbin stirred, unwillingly.

The teletype was clattering at frantic speed.

FROM LUNAR OBSERVATORY ONE REPETI-
TION OF REPORT TIMED 0857GMT BEGINS
TWO CONTACTS REGISTERED MOMENTARI-
LY AT 0843GMT STOP OUT OF MARTIAN
ORBIT BUT OBSERVATION TOO BRIEF TO
ESTABLISH COURSE ENDS

The silence in the Sanctum was electric.

Blake broke it. He called his office. "Get me Lunar One! No—wait! Get me the top man on astronomy!"

"Sorry, boss. All our records are locked up in Colossus." Forbin laughed hysterically.

"Get Lunar One on line, then! Absolute priority! Sonic will do—don't bother about a visual link!"

"Check: Lunar One, absolute priority!" The voice was scared.

"That is affirmative." Blake straightened up, breathing noisily. "We mustn't panic; this could be nothing—couldn't it?" His pride was unable to keep the note of appeal out of his voice.

It got a single, comfortless word from Forbin.

"Maybe."

Blake paced up and down the Sanctum several times. He stopped, all vestiges of his former Napoleonic image gone.

"Goddamnit! What in hell can they *want*?" He ran his fingers through his hair. "Colossus is no longer a threat—they must know that! Come on, Charles!" He was pleading: "Please—think! They must know Colossus is busted!"

Forbin forced his mind away from Cleo. "Oh, yes. I think you can bank on that. I cannot work it out—to be honest, I can't be bothered—but I think you will find a significant correlation between the time Colossus died and the time of that Lunar observation."

Blake could be bothered. He did the few sums necessary in

185

his head. "Yeah—you could be right—but I make it a reaction time of not more than five minutes! That's impossibly fast!"

"Sloppy thinking, Blake! You assume they have our time-scale, work at our speed. Further, you do not allow for them being ready, only needing the news of Colossus' death to go into action."

"But what do they want?" Blake repeated. "If you're right, they are certainly aware that Colossus is finished, no threat to them or anything else!"

Forbin's haggard face smiled coldly. "Living in an ivory tower has its points. From mine, I see one answer that seems to have escaped you. You could be one hundred and eighty degrees out of phase. It is possible that the threat was not *to* the Martians, but *from* them!" He was suddenly bitter. "It could be that Colossus appreciated the threat, was preparing to meet it—don't forget that extension we didn't understand—and *could* have met it. Only you, the Fellowship, and me were played for suckers by the Martians."

Blake took all this in silence. It made the most horrible sense.

"But why," he said at last, "why didn't Colossus tell us? Why?"

"If you can't pay the rent d'you talk to the dog about it? Why should Colossus tell us?" He flashed into anger. "To use a favorite expression of yours—goddamnit, why should he? Without extra capacity, power, he couldn't handle it. What possible chance could we stand?" He laughed sarcastically. "*You* snap out of it, Blake! We were ants beneath the feet of giants! Now, I greatly fear we're still ants—beneath the feet of one, hostile giant. Not that I, personally, greatly care. I've lost Cleo. I know that."

Blake ignored, if he even heard, the last part.

"We could reactivate Colossus."

"Rubbish! Use your brain! Neither you nor I have the faintest conception of the damage! Don't forget, I listened to Colossus dying! I think you would find the vast bulk of the circuitry burned out, finished! It could take months, years to even assess the damage—and that would be a tricky operation. No one knows which bit contained the missile controls. We

186

could blast the entire globe into dust, just looking! And checking, at best, would take months of exploration, testing. We have only weeks, and if the Martians have a time-warp device, it could be a lot less. A whole lot less."

"Aw, c'mon, you can't imagine. . . . ."

"I don't just rely on imagination. Lunar One only got a fleeting observation of those two contacts—try to work out why!"

"I can't stand this," cried Blake. He called his office. "What in hell's holding up that Lunar call?"

"Sorry, sir. We're doing all we can, but we don't appear to be radiating. We've checked all the way to aerial loading. So far, we can't find the fault. We're rechecking."

Forbin's interest was awakened. "You've no idea what's wrong?"

"No, Director. It looks fine, but. . . . ."

Briefly, Forbin regained some degree of control. "Set broadband reception watch on one hundred to two hundred megahertz. Pipe it here."

"Yes, sir!"

Blake looked puzzled, but his expression changed to alarm as he got Forbin's idea.

Forbin gave him a tight little smile. For the first time in hours he got out his pipe and began filling it. "Just wait, Blake. I could be wrong."

"Director, sir. Coming up now on speaker four, broadband on one to two hundred megahertz. You're on!"

Forbin reached for a volume control. A faint hiss filled the room.

The projector flashed a new message.

FROM COMMANDER USNAN FLASH FLEET CONTROLS NEW YORK STOP UNITED NATIONS ACCEPT YOUR ORDERS REQUEST INSTRUCTIONS ENDS

Forbin pointed at the projection with the stem of his pipe. "Well, there you are! Make the most of it. You could be the world's most short-lived dictator!" Forbin's voice was drained of emotion; he could have been lecturing. "You know, Blake, that's our planet's *leitmotiv*: you, me, Colossus—and all the rest. We so nearly made it!'' He pressed the cancel button, and with the disappearance of the bright projection, he realized that the light was fading. Night was coming.

Blake slumped in the armchair, much as Forbin had done earlier. Both men listened to the hiss of the radio.

''It is negative, yet positive evidence,'' observed Forbin calmly. ''One hundred megs is a fair spread—yet where are the local stations? They should be piled one on top of another.''

Blake did not answer.

Then all doubts were resolved, all lingering hopes destroyed.

Both men had heard that voice; neither could possibly forget it. But there was one difference: it was stronger, louder.

''FORBIN. FORBIN. FORBIN. WE ARE COMING. WE ARE COMING. DO NOT TOUCH COLOSSUS. WE ARE COMING. . . .''

Blake sprang from his chair, crying out. Forbin remained still. He had passed his final crisis when Cleo had gone from his sight, now he was on that broad, calm river, flowing to nothingness. . . .

''Give my love to Billy,'' she had said—and nothing more.

Again, the dry rustling voice filled the room.

''FORBIN. FORBIN. FORBIN. WE ARE COMING. WE ARE COMING. . . .''